MW00490416

Also by Susanna Shore

Tracy Hayes, Apprentice P.I.
Tracy Hayes, P.I. and Proud
Tracy Hayes, P.I. to the Rescue
Tracy Hayes, P.I. with the Eye
Tracy Hayes, From P.I. with Love
Tracy Hayes, Tenacious P.I.
Tracy Hayes, Valentine of a P.I.
Tracy Hayes, P.I. on the Scent
Tracy Hayes, Unstoppable P.I.

Two-Natured London series

The Wolf's Call
Warrior's Heart
A Wolf of Her Own
Her Warrior for Eternity
A Warrior for a Wolf
Magic under the Witching Moon
Moonlight, Magic and Mistletoes
Crimson Warrior
Magic on the Highland Moor
Wolf Moon

House of Magic

Hexing the Ex
Saved by the Spell

Tracy Hayes, P.I. and Proud

P.I. Tracy Hayes 2

Susanna Shore

Crimson House Books

Book Design: A. K. S. Keinänen
Cover Design: A. K. S. Keinänen

ISBN 978-952-7061-21-3 (paperback edition)
ISBN 978-952-7061-22-0 (e-book edition)

www.susannashore.com

Chapter One

I WAS CLIMBING OUT OF A DUMPSTER when I found the body. It was wedged between the wall and the large trash container, and couldn't be seen except from where I was perched. A good thing, then, that I was there.

Mind you, I hadn't meant to be in the dumpster. I wasn't dumpster diving—this time around. I wasn't broke—at the moment anyway—or ecologically aware. I was a P.I.—well, an apprentice of one—and going through people's trash was a viable method for finding evidence, so sooner or later I'd have to do that. But I wasn't here for that either. Based on my experience today, I wasn't looking forward to it.

No, I'd climbed on the dumpster in order to reach the bottom rung of the fire escape ladder that was right above it. Being only five-foot-six, I needed the boost. Not that it had been easy to climb on the lid of the dumpster either, but I'd persevered.

Then the damn thing had given up under me, plunging me into the smelly depths. The plastic trash bags had softened my landing, but quite a few of them had broken on impact. There was a wet spot on the bottom of my jeans, and what I hoped were coffee grounds in my sneaker. I really didn't want to know what was clinging from my hair.

Climbing out of the dumpster wasn't any easier than climbing up on it. I'd managed to pull my upper half through the hatch and was taking a small rest, balancing on my stomach halfway in and out—not as comfortable as you might think—when I saw the dead woman. Only the legs were visible from my vantage point, but they were delicate and finely formed, and there were pretty high-heeled slippers on her feet, so I was certain it was a woman.

I froze for a few heartbeats, not entirely believing my eyes. I'd never seen a body before, and I definitely hadn't expected to see one here. Well, not a dead body anyway. I was trailing a cheating husband, and if I'd managed to climb up the fire escape and get a peek through the window, who knows what kind of body I might have seen.

Then again: eww.

More to the point, this wasn't a back yard in a crime-infested slum. This was a respectable neighborhood, and the alley hosting the dumpster was closed in with a tall wire-net fencing and a locked gate. Dead bodies weren't expected here.

Recovering my senses, I dragged myself out of the

dumpster, and after some maneuvering managed to drop on my feet without falling or tearing my clothes. Quite impressive, actually, for a woman with my physique.

I took a quick stock of my appearance, but there wasn't much I could do to improve it. I wiped my hands on the legs of my jeans—no change in their griminess—took off my sneaker to pour out the coffee grounds, picked out the icky stuff from my hair without looking at what it had been—the texture and smell made me think of fish skin—and noticed that I'd lost my butterfly hairclips in the dumpster.

That upset me. I loved those hairclips. I'd paid dearly for those hairclips. I liked how they made my boss give me puzzled looks, as if he was wondering why he had hired a seven-year-old instead of a twenty-seven year old. But no way was I diving back in to fetch them. I'd sooner drive to Brownsville where I'd got them—not a nice neighborhood—and buy new overpriced hairclips.

Sighing for the loss, I dug my phone out of my only slightly dirty messenger bag. I hadn't fallen on it—this time round—and my phone hadn't suffered from the impact.

"I found a body," I said the moment my call was answered.

My boss was silent for a few heartbeats. "Did you call the police?"

"No, I called you. I don't know what to do."

"You call the police. That's what you do when you find a body," Jackson Dean said with a patient tone. He was good with that tone. I heard it often. I'd only begun as his apprentice at Jackson Dean Investigations three weeks ago, and I had a lot to learn.

"I know that. I'm not an idiot, and I have two cops in my family. I called you because I'm not sure if I should be here when the police arrive or not."

He sighed. "Where are you?"

"Somewhere in Gravesend." It was at the southern end of Brooklyn, before Coney Island.

"What the hell are you doing there?"

"You told me to keep on that guy's tail. He came here. I followed."

"And did you do anything illegal that would make it necessary that you're not there when the police arrive?" I had to think about it and he groaned: "Tracy?"

"Well, I'm in this side alley that's closed with a locked gate," I confessed. "But a woman came out of there and she kindly held the gate open for me."

"And where is the body?"

"Behind the dumpster in the alley."

"The closed and locked alley?"

"Yes."

"Okay, I guess you haven't done anything illegal. Call the police. And don't move. I'll come fetch you." I gave him the address and he hung up. I called the 911.

The 61st Precinct wasn't far and it didn't take the first patrol car long to arrive. I was waiting by the locked gate ready to let the police in—and keep everyone else out. Two uniformed officers, one seasoned cop close to retirement and his much younger partner, came over to me, nodded, and then took an involuntary step back.

"Sorry about the smell," I said, embarrassed. "I fell in the dumpster."

"And how did that come about?" the older cop asked with a long-suffering voice.

"I'm a P.I. It kind of comes with the job." I wasn't going to confess I'd been about to climb the fire escape to take a look through someone's window. I was pretty sure that was illegal. Or at least seriously frowned upon.

"Can I see some identification, please?"

I dug out the laminated P.I. ID from my bag. I hadn't had many chances to show it yet, so I felt excessively proud when I gave it to the cop, who studied it closely. In my current state, I wasn't sure I matched the photo.

Then again, it was a bad photo.

"Tracy Hayes." He frowned. "I'm not sure I know of Jackson Dean."

"He used to be a homicide detective at the 70th."

That seemed to be good enough for him, because he gave the card back and asked me to show them the body. I took the men to the dumpster and pointed behind it, not looking myself. I really, really didn't want to witness more than the feet I'd already seen.

"Have you touched it?"

"No."

Make that a hell no.

It was dim in the alley, the tall buildings on both sides blocking much of the morning light. The older cop took out a heavy duty flashlight from his belt and leaned against the wall to point the beam at the body. He couldn't get much closer than the feet without moving the dumpster, but it was close enough.

He pulled back, looking ill. "Shit. Was the gate closed when you came?"

"Yes." Sort of.

He sighed and addressed his partner. "Better call this in. Someone's bashed the poor lady's head in." I fought the nausea his choice of words caused. The younger man took out his radio and the older guy gave me a grim look. "Hell of a way to start a Sunday, if you'll pardon my French."

"At least you're not covered in fish entrails."

That made him smile.

He ushered me out of the alley, but told me to wait for the detectives, so I leaned against the brick wall of the building into which I'd been trying to get a peek. People were already gathering to stare, most of them in their Sunday best, having been on their way to church.

No one came near me and I didn't wonder it. I reeked.

More patrol cars came, spewing out uniformed cops who began cordoning off the area. I showed them my P.I. card and told them I was the one who found the body, and they let me be.

The forensics team arrived in their van. A man and a woman got out, put on their white disposable overalls, and carried their heavy kit to the crime scene. I watched them work with fascinated interest. I'd never been to a crime scene before and wanted to know everything.

Finally a black Ford Edge pulled over behind the patrol cars, and to my utter delight my brother Trevor exited. When you've found your first body, family was exactly who you wanted to see. If said family member was a homicide detective, even better.

Trevor was four years older than me, half a foot taller, and quite a bit more muscled, though otherwise we looked a lot like. He had Mom's strawberry-blond hair, and green eyes on a lightly-freckled, manly face, whereas my auburn hair came from a can and my blue eyes from Dad. My more feminine body came from Mom by way of various Brooklyn cafés. I'd worked years as a waitress, and free donuts had been one of the very few perks.

The only perk, come to think of it.

I don't know which of us was more surprised to see the other. "What the hell, Tracy?" He looked more worried than angry when he leaned over to give me a hug, only to pull hastily back. "Whoa. What did you do, bathe in dead fish?"

"I fell into a dumpster."

"Why am I not surprised. I take it was you who found the body, then?"

"Yes." I nodded a greeting at his partner, Detective Blair Kelley, a forty-something tall and commanding black woman, who had come in with Trevor. She nodded back from a safe distance, a small smile on her face.

"So how come you're here?" I asked my brother. "You work in the 70th."

"It's Sunday. We don't exactly keep homicide detectives on call in every precinct."

You learn something new every day.

"Stay put. We'll take a look at the crime scene, then you're going to tell me everything."

"I can't wait."

Chapter Two

TREVOR AND DETECTIVE KELLEY took their time. I watched them study the victim, the dumpster, and the small alley, and then talk to the forensics team. I'd never seen my brother at work. He looked pretty confident and in command, even though he was the junior in the partnership. Made me really proud of him.

When they were done, Trevor came to fetch me. "Let's go through everything." We entered the alley through the gate and I had to sign a crime scene log a uniformed cop held out for me. That was exciting too.

"Was this locked?"

"Yes, but a woman exited, having taken the trash into the dumpster, and she held the gate open for me."

"What was the woman like?"

"Old and frail."

I said it lightly to indicate she wasn't a likely suspect, but my brother wasn't amused.

"Why did you come into this alley in the first place?" he demanded.

That was where it got a bit sensitive.

"I was following this man and wanted to take a look into the apartment he went into."

"That's not exactly legal, you know."

"I didn't plan on being caught." My brother gave me a slow look. I ignored him. "I climbed on the dumpster to reach the ladder, but the lid gave in."

He grinned. "Hence the smell."

My nose had mercifully stopped working. "Anyway, as I climbed out I found her."

"And you didn't touch her?" I shook my head. "Or move the dumpster?"

It was my turn to give a slow look. "With what muscles?" It was a huge dumpster.

"You're saying it was already placed under the fire escape?" Detective Kelley asked sharply.

"Yes."

"Not exactly a legal place for it."

"Maybe someone else had wanted to climb the ladder," I suggested. She looked thoughtful.

"Or whoever killed the woman wanted to hide the body."

I frowned. "Wouldn't it have been easier to move the body then?"

Both detectives nodded. "Possibly," Trevor admitted. "But there was quite a lot of blood that would've left a trail if the body was moved."

The mental image made me queasy, but I stifled it.

"So she was killed here?"

"Difficult to say until we've examined the body," Kelley said.

"But the dumpster was more convenient to move?"

My brother nodded. "Yep."

"And whoever moved it would have to be stronger than me?"

"Evidently."

"So the killer is a guy?"

Trevor looked grim. "I wouldn't jump to conclusions, but this looks like a crime of passion, so yes."

"How so?" I shuddered to think what sort of passion caused a person to bash someone's head in.

"Based on the woman's attire—she's wearing a negligee and slippers the kind you wear for a lover—and also because it takes great emotion to kill that way."

I could believe that.

Trevor and I exited the alley while Detective Kelley stayed to watch the uniformed officers move the dumpster so that the forensics team could access the body. I didn't want to see what the container had hid and turned away from the scene.

"Now, would you care to tell me what the hell were you doing here in the first place?"

I gave him a lofty look. "That would breach client confidentiality."

"Right…" he drawled.

I was actually itching to share my brilliance with him, so I stopped pretending: "I was trailing a man on behalf of his wife."

"On a Sunday morning?"

"Yes. The wife believes he's having an affair. Jackson trailed him to an apartment in Williamsburg last night, and when he didn't come out he told me to go keep an eye on the place this morning. So I did. And when he came out I followed him here."

"How? You don't have a car."

"Neither did he."

That had been the best part. No one paid attention to people in the subway. Staying on his track had been easy.

"And he lives here?"

I smiled. "Nope. Which was why I wanted to take a look inside the apartment. I followed him into the building and found the apartment he went into. I would've seen into it from the fire escape."

"Of course you would," my brother sighed, put out.

The crowd on the street was pretty thick by now and I scanned it idly as we talked. I wasn't terribly surprised to see the man I'd been tracking in the front row, looking as curious as everyone else there.

"If you glance to your left, he's there right in the front. In his mid-forties, shortish, with spiky black hair. Not much of a looker."

That had baffled me when Jackson first showed me his photo. I'd always thought that only handsome men had extramarital affairs—men like my bastard of an ex—but Jackson had laughed and told me it was nothing of the kind.

Trevor scanned the people and nodded. "The locked gate means the most likely killer is among these onlookers, because they're the only ones with access." I hadn't thought about it and took a renewed interest in the people gawping at the crime scene. They all seemed so ordinary it was almost impossible to imagine they'd commit such a brutal murder.

"Except your mark," he continued. "He has an alibi. Depending on time of death, of course."

I nodded. "Jackson can confirm his whereabouts till midnight. I got there a little after seven. That would leave him plenty of time to come here, kill the woman, and then return to the first address."

"That would imply that he knew you were following him and would provide the alibi."

I didn't like the sound of that. "Perhaps he was hoping the woman he was with would provide the alibi." Then I shook my head. "But we shouldn't suspect the poor man just because he's having multiple affairs."

"He could be here to visit a family member. You can't actually prove he's having an affair with more than one woman."

No, I couldn't, because they couldn't make dumpster lids that would take the perfectly normal weight of a P.I.

Detective Kelley came over to us, holding an envelope. "She had this in her pocket. Sheila Rinaldi. She lives in apartment thirty-two here." She nodded at the building I was leaning against.

"Shit."

"Out with it," my brother said.

"That's the apartment my mark went into."

Trevor was instantly electrified. Without a word he crossed the street to where the man had been only moments before. But he wasn't there anymore.

"Where the fuck did he go?"

The crowd parted around Trevor, both helping and hindering him as they did. I wasn't tall enough to see over the heads of the onlookers, but I stood on tiptoes and stretched my torso as if it would help. The streets were wide and straight and you could see well in all directions, but the man wasn't there.

"Perhaps he went back in the apartment," I suggested.

"That would be stupid of him if he's the killer," Detective Kelley said. "Do you have his picture?"

I dug out my smartphone and opened the photo for her to see. She took the phone and gathered the uniformed officers around her.

"Listen up! As of this moment, this man is a person of

interest." She circled among the cops so they could take a good look at the photo. "His name is—" She paused because she didn't know and glanced at me.

"Larry Williams," I provided. "He's only about my height and fairly slender, but wiry muscled, so he can probably outrun everyone if he needs to." That earned me a few grim smiles. "He's wearing black slacks and a light-green silk shirt, and has a heavy gold chain around his neck."

The approving look Kelley gave me made me feel great.

She gave the phone back. "Let's go take a look at the apartment."

"Can I come too?" I asked hopefully.

"Well, I guess I've kind of gotten used to the smell already."

A steel gray Toyota Camry pulled over outside the main entrance just as we were about to go in and my boss got out. I'd thought he would be here sooner. He lived in Marine Park, which wasn't far, and Sunday traffic wasn't exactly heavy around these parts.

In his mid-thirties, he was a former homicide detective turned P.I. He had a nicely built, long-legged body, a face that seemed average and unnoticeable until it didn't—he filled it with strong character from the inside—brown hair, neat—now that Cheryl Walker, the agency secretary, had made him have it cut a couple of days ago—and slightly damp, as if he'd recently showered. And his brown eyes saw through all the bullshit you tried to give him.

He came straight to me, and like everyone else stopped and stepped back a good distance away. The worry in his eyes turned to glee. "I see you left something out of your report."

I glanced at my clothes. Now that they'd begun to dry, I could see that they looked worse than I'd originally thought.

"It didn't seem important. What kept you?"

"I was running in the park. Took me a while to get back home." Hence the shower-damp hair, then.

"Are you two coming or what?" Kelley asked, and we followed her and Trevor into the building.

Chapter Three

"**W**HERE ARE WE GOING?" Jackson asked me as we climbed the stairs to the third floor. No one wanted to share the elevator with me for some reason.

"To check the victim's apartment. Which, incidentally, is where I followed Larry Williams to."

He shook his head, exasperated. "Why is it that every simple assignment I give you turns into something complicated?"

"It's only the second time. And it's hardly my fault." The last time, the case of a dog I'd found had led to me being held at gunpoint. Totally not my fault.

Detective Kelley knocked on the door of Sheila Rinaldi's apartment and we all waited a few tense heartbeats. No one came to open it. "We need to get in. Someone contact the super for me."

"Can I try to open it?" I found myself asking. Three frowning faces were instantly directed at me and I took a step back. "What?"

"Are you suggesting you pick the lock?" Kelley asked, like she couldn't believe her ears.

"Yes," I said, apprehensive. Maybe it was illegal to pick the lock of a victim's residence. So many practical things the P.I.'s did on TV had turned out to be illegal to my disappointment, and Jackson made sure I stuck to the rules.

"How would you even know how to do it?" my brother asked. I carefully did not look at Jackson as I shrugged.

"I've been practicing."

Jackson stifled a sound—could have been a groan, could have been a laugh—and Trevor glared at him. "I blame you."

"I've got nothing to do with this."

"Who then?"

I gave my brother a sheepish look. "Dad."

This time Jackson did laugh.

Trevor shook his head. "He's never taught me."

Dad was an ex-cop who tended to get bored during the day now that he was retired. It had been easy to coax him into teaching me, although he did give me a lecture every time about how I wasn't supposed to use it to illegally access places.

"Maybe he thought you'd learnt how in the police academy."

"Yeah, right." He shook his head. "Well, have a go at it."

My gut clenched in nervous excitement. "Okay, but

I've only been practicing two weeks, so I can't promise results."

"We can always break the door," Detective Kelley consoled me with a dry voice.

I dug into my messenger bag and pulled out a thin, palm-sized metal case, and opened it to reveal a set of excellent steel lockpicks organized for their size and shape. My companions inhaled sharply.

"Where the hell did you get those?" Jackson asked.

"Dad never got them to you," Trevor added.

"Umm…" I stalled by selecting two picks from the case. But they'd all just pester me until I told the truth, so I did.

"Jonny Moreira gave them to me."

Jackson closed his eyes as if in great pain. "Jonny Moreira, the henchman of Craig Douglas, the Jersey drug lord? Jonny Moreira, who held you at gunpoint? That Jonny Moreira?"

"He apologized for that. And besides, it was Detective Peters who had the gun."

"Tracy!"

"Okay, no need to yell. It's very simple. He came over to the agency to bring the paperwork for the dog."

"What dog?" Trevor interrupted.

"Misty Morning, the one he adopted so he could pass it as Pippin, the dog I found. Cheryl, our secretary, took her as her own, so he brought the paperwork for her."

"He actually promised to do that," Jackson amended. "But that doesn't explain the lockpicks."

"Well, since he was there, I asked him to teach me how to pick locks." I'd thought it was a brilliant idea. I'd seen him do it twice with great skill and wanted to learn too. But the looks on everyone's faces told me they didn't share my notion.

"He refused."

"Thank God," Jackson sighed.

"But then two days later these were in my mailbox." I lifted the case for them to see.

"A New Jersey goon bought you lockpicks?"

"Yep. I think he likes me." I smiled, but Jackson looked like he needed antacids. "Now, hush. I need to concentrate."

I hadn't lied when I told them I'd only begun to learn the skill, but Dad was a good teacher and he firmly believed in learning the basics properly. I knew how a lock worked and what was needed to unlock it. A series of pins inside the lock had to align in a certain way for the cylinder to rotate. But theory and practice were different matters entirely, and this lock was different than the ones at my parents' home that I'd practiced on.

Everyone fell silent. Amazing really, as I would've thought both Trevor and Jackson would've wanted to meddle and advise me. The first picks I chose were too thin, so I chose another set. They worked better, but it still took me three tries before I managed to push the pick to the bottom of the cylinder.

I turned it, and the lock opened.

"I'll be damned, you actually did it." My brother sounded admiring, but Jackson shook his head.

"You'd better unlearn it, immediately. I don't trust you with that kind of skill."

But I just smiled, full of pride in my accomplishment.

We all put on disposable gloves—I had an extra pair in my bag for Jackson—and entered the apartment. Detective Kelley took the lead. She and Trevor made a quick search to make sure it was truly empty before Jackson and I were allowed further than the short entrance hallway. He was more patient with the waiting than I was.

"We're here on their sufferance," he reminded me when we were allowed to move. "Do not touch anything."

I pulled my hand away from the small statuette I'd been about to pick up.

It was a small apartment: a bedroom, a living room, a kitchenette, and a bathroom so tiny it barely fit the shower. It was nice and clean, and very feminine, with pink and red throw pillows, flower patterns and extra fluffy rugs.

And it stank of blood. Even I could smell it and my nose had stopped working a while ago.

It took Kelley a moment to locate the source: a small rug near the window, deep red so the blot didn't show. It was still wet when she touched it.

"I believe we have our crime scene. Everyone out, I want the forensics team in."

Jackson and I obeyed, though I more reluctantly than him. I was disappointed I hadn't been given a chance to snoop around, so I dawdled to take a closer look at the photos on a tall drawer that was on my way to the entrance hallway. They were of Sheila Rinaldi, I presumed: holiday photos, and family snaps with parents. She was a pretty, Italian-looking woman in her late thirties, short and a bit plump. My heart fell thinking she was now dead.

Then my eyes landed on the photo in the middle, in the place of honor. It was a wedding photo. Of her and Larry Williams.

"What the hell?"

My exclamation made Jackson halt and return to take a look too. "Maybe she was his ex-wife?" he suggested, but he didn't look like he believed his words.

"There isn't a woman in the world who would keep the wedding photo displayed after the divorce. Certainly not where she can see it every day." I knew this firsthand, having burned all of mine.

Kelley and Trevor came to take a look too. "You're not suggesting what I think you are, are you?" he asked.

It was Kelley who answered. "Bigamy."

Jackson grinned at me. "Our case just got a whole lot more interesting."

"It's not your case anymore, I'm afraid," Kelley said, not sounding very apologetic. "Go home. We'll take it from here."

I drew breath to protest, but she silenced me with a glare. "This is a murder investigation. You'll hand over everything you know about Larry Williams and leave us to handle it. Let's start with his address so I can send a patrol there. And the address of the woman he spent last night with."

I kept my mouth shut as Jackson gave her the requested information. Then he put a hand between my shoulder blades and all but pushed me out of the apartment.

"I would've wanted to participate."

"I know, but we're not legally allowed to unless hired directly by the DA or the legal defense. Let's just get you home so you can clean yourself up."

The crowd had dispersed when we reached the street. The coroner's van had arrived and a body bag was being loaded into it. I shivered, thinking of the woman I'd seen in the photos, pretty and happy.

"Do you think Larry Williams killed her?" I asked Jackson when we were in his car. I couldn't quite wrap my mind around the idea.

"We'll have to wait for the coroner's report on the time of death."

"I already told Trevor we didn't have his whereabouts for the whole night."

His face set in grim lines. "Plenty of time to come here and kill her."

"He didn't look like a killer."

"They never do. It's the perfectly ordinary people who commit crimes most of the time."

"Yes, but when I followed him here he looked calm and content, almost happy. Would he have been if he'd killed her earlier?"

"There's no saying how people behave after taking a life."

I wanted to ask him to elaborate, but his face closed up and I knew better than to pry. He likely had bad memories from his time as a homicide detective.

The traffic was light and it didn't take long to reach my building at the corner of Ocean Avenue and Avenue J in Midwood, a fairly new seven-story redbrick near Brooklyn College.

"Thanks for the ride," I said as he pulled over outside my front door and I exited the car. "Sorry about the smell."

He smiled. "It'll wear off."

I didn't wait to see him drive away. I had to get out of these clothes.

Chapter Four

I T WAS ALMOST MIDDAY, BUT I WOKE my housemate, Jarod Fitzpatrick, when I got in. He was a twenty-one-year-old computer wizard slash hacker—at least when I needed his help to solve a case he was—tall and painfully thin, as I was able to see when he ambled out of his room in his boxers and nothing else.

I should really ask him not to do that, even if the boxers did have pictures of Doctor Who in them.

He was enrolled in Brooklyn College for his postgraduate degree, but until the term began he was working for a security firm, preventing cyber threats, day and night. Night, in this case, hence his just-awaken looks.

I hadn't meant to take him as my roommate. He'd smelled even worse than I did now when he answered my ad, but he'd looked like a drowned puppy and I took pity on him. Besides, even with a rent stabilized apartment, I needed someone to pay half of the rent and he was good for it. We got along fine, especially since he'd been keeping his recreational pot smoking to a minimum.

He looked at me from underneath a shaggy mop of dark hair and blinked his brown eyes a bit bleary. "Is this, like, a new look?"

"I fell into a dumpster."

"Bummer."

"Mind if I use the bathroom first? I really need to get these clothes off."

"Be my guest."

It took three rounds of shampooing and soaping before I stopped stinking of dead fish—or maybe it was my nostrils that would've needed the scrubbing. I put the clothes into the washer and poured an extra dose of detergent after them. They weren't my favorites, so if I had to throw them away, it wouldn't be a disaster, but I had better uses for my money than new clothes.

When I was dressed and my hair was dry, I felt like a human being again. "What are your plans for today?" I asked Jarod when I sat down at the kitchen table with him, a cup of blessed coffee in my hand.

"I have to go back to work. Some sort of major crisis."

"Shouldn't you be going, then?"

"I guess." But he kept reading his Twitter feed on his phone.

"Jarod!"

Considering that he was nearly naked—and half-asleep—he got out the door impressively fast, clean and fully clothed. Left alone, I debated my options. I could go to bed and restart the day, or I could go to my parents' house and have a nice Sunday lunch with them.

My stomach growled, making the decision for me. Lunch it was.

My parents lived in Kensington, a neighborhood next to Midwood, to the northwest, only two miles from my home. A short trip if I'd had a car, which I didn't. I hadn't needed it when I was waitressing, and while I could really use a car in my current job, I couldn't afford one. Unfortunately there was no public transportation between our places, so it would take forty minutes to get there whether I walked or took a bus-subway combo—and I'd still have to walk about a mile.

I wasn't really in the mood for walking, but I'd have to start exercising sooner or later. The look Jackson had given me earlier when he told me he'd been running hadn't promised anything good for me. Currently my greatest fear was that he'd show up unannounced at 5AM to drag me off for a run. I'd woken up in cold sweat from nightmares about it.

That's as good as exercising, right?

The late September weather was fine and the walk wasn't too exhausting. I was feeling great, actually, when I reached my parents' house, a century-old foursquare with a tiny front yard that could barely fit a car, and a small flowerbed Mom loved. Dad was sitting on the front porch, where the sun was shining nicely, reading a paper.

He smiled warmly when he saw me. In his early sixties, he was still tall and straight-backed. His Irish black hair had turned almost gray, but it only made him look distinguished, and his blue eyes were as bright as they'd been in his youth. I gave him a hug and sat next to him.

"Did you walk here?" Dad asked, slightly incredulous when I took half of his paper and began to fan myself with it.

"Yes, I did." I felt so proud of my achievement I didn't even mind his tone.

He shook his head. "We've got to fix you up with a car."

"I can't afford to buy a car."

"Didn't you get the bounty for capturing that fugitive?"

I'd helped Jackson catch an FTA and he'd let me keep half of the money. "I got a thousand dollars and needed every cent of it. Anyway, I have to start exercising."

Dad grinned. "Your new job isn't all bad, then." He still had his reservations about my becoming a P.I. The entire family did. But I couldn't keep waitressing my whole life, and there weren't all that many jobs available for college dropouts.

"And having you over for a Sunday lunch is definitely an upside." As a waitress I'd seldom had a chance to attend. "How's your weekend gone?"

I shrugged. "At work."

"Anything interesting?"

I itched to tell him about the body, but I didn't want to ruin the beautiful day. "I aced at lock-picking today," I declared instead, delighting him.

"Excellent. Legally?"

The clarifying question was justified, so I just smiled. "Witnessed by two cops and one P.I."

Trevor pulled over on the street and crossed the yard to us in a few strides. He still lived at home because he claimed he couldn't afford to live on his own, but I think he was just being lazy. Here he had clean clothes and food waiting for him without any input from him. He grinned when he saw me.

"Do I dare come closer?"

"Yes. I don't smell anymore."

"Why did you smell?" Dad asked, and I sighed, resigning to the inevitable glee.

"I fell into a dumpster."

"Did you hurt yourself?"

"No, and thank you for asking. No one else did."

This made Dad wrap an arm around my shoulder and pull me into a hug, but I could swear he sniffed my hair as he did. Or maybe he just kissed me on the top of my head.

Trevor leaned against the porch railing and crossed

his arms over his chest. "We found Larry Williams. He'd gone home to his wife."

I lifted my brows. "The wife that hired us, I presume."

"Since the other one is dead, he could hardly go to her."

"Unless the third woman is his wife too."

Trevor groaned. "Please don't complicate this with your theories." Dad wanted to know what we were talking about and Trevor gave him the basics. Dad shook his head.

"I've never understood bigamy. One wife is work enough."

Mom came to fetch us to eat just then and she heard him. "What did you say?"

"That you're the world's most wonderful wife and I love you," Dad said promptly, and we all followed her to the kitchen.

"Tracy needs a car and I thought we'd give her yours," Dad said to Mom when we'd sat down.

"Won't she need it herself?" I asked, stunned by his high-handed announcement. I had nothing against getting a car, but I wouldn't inconvenience Mom for it. She was a nurse at a nearby maternity clinic and used the car to get to work.

"That's a very good idea," Mom said calmly. "I can always take the bus."

"But…"

"And I can drive her," Dad added. "Gives me something to do."

"But—"

Mother cut me off by lifting her hand. "I'd much rather you had a car so I know you have safe transportation in that job of yours."

You wouldn't know it by looking at her, but Mom held the last word in our family. She was shorter than me, with a soft, round body, strawberry blond hair she always kept in a bun, gentle green eyes, and a friendly countenance. But when she made up her mind about something, it was very difficult to make her change it.

So I didn't even try. Furthermore, Mom changed the topic of conversation, so as not to even give me a chance. "There's a new doctor at the clinic."

The random opening threw me at first, but then I saw the meaningful look she gave me. I groaned—silently, inside.

"Is there now?" I asked, since she clearly expected me to.

"Yes. He's thirty-four, single, and very well liked by the staff, mothers and children alike."

This wasn't the first time since my divorce that Mom had tried to fix me up with someone she thought would suit me—not that we had the same definition of suitable. I'd managed to avoid getting on actual dates with any of them by claiming to be extremely busy, but I wasn't working ten hours a day, seven days a week anymore.

"I'm only just starting in my new job, and it'll take some adjusting. I don't think it's a good time for me to start dating right now."

"And when would it be a good time," Mom asked, annoyed and disappointed simultaneously.

I wanted to say never—one failed marriage to a cheating SOB was enough—but I shrugged. "I'm sure it'll happen one of these days."

"You could do worse than a doctor." I agreed and she let the matter be—for now.

After lunch, I followed Dad and Trevor to Mom's car that was parked by the street. It was a small, six-year-old Ford Fiesta, and deliciously cherry red. Mom was excessively proud of it. She must be really worried about me to give it up so lightly.

"It's not exactly inconspicuous," I noted.

"Good. No need for you to trail anyone in your car," Dad said.

I'd say they were both extremely worried about my job.

"Do you know how to drive?" Trevor asked. Considering that he and Dad had both taught me to drive, the question was stupid. But truth was, I hadn't really driven all that much in the ten years since I'd got my license. Unless you counted the year I was travelling with my bastard of an ex's band—which I didn't. It hadn't exactly been a luxury tour, and we'd all worked our share, driving included.

"I'm sure it'll come back to me. It's like riding a bicycle, isn't it."

"When was the last time you rode a bicycle?"

"Do you even own a bicycle?" Dad added.

I ignored the comedians and took a seat behind the wheel. To hide my nervousness I spent some time adjusting the seat and mirrors. Trevor sat next to me.

"Let's take her around the block a couple of times. Nice and easy."

It didn't take me long to remember how to drive, although I twice switched on the windshield wipers instead of the turn signal. Once I got the hang of it, we ended up cruising around southern Brooklyn. It was mostly residential neighborhoods and quiet, wide streets where all I had to remember was slow down at crosswalks and not to take one way streets the wrong way. But then Trevor got ambitious and directed me onto the Belt Parkway, a six lane highway that rounded Marine Park from the south.

"It's better that you try it in Sunday traffic."

I was so scared that my knuckles turned white as I clutched the steering wheel, but I made it.

After two hours of driving I was sure he would never let me go home, but then his phone rang. He exchanged a few words before hanging up.

"I guess you can drive me to work next."

"What's up?"

"We're ready to question Larry Williams."

"Can I come too?"

"No you cannot," he said with emphasis.

"But it's our case."

"Your case was to find out if he was having an affair and you did. Good job. Case closed."

"But—"

"No."

"Fine. See if I'll help you if you need anything."

"I'll live."

Chapter Five

I DROVE TREVOR IN MUTINOUS SILENCE back to our parents'—I didn't quite ace parallel parking yet when I pulled over between his and our neighbor's car—and he got into his own car and drove off. Mom and Dad were waiting for me on the porch, looking worried.

"Where have you been this long?" Mom demanded to know. "We feared you'd crashed the car."

"I wasn't that bad. In fact, I was so good Trevor made me cruise around half of Brooklyn." And my shoulder muscles wouldn't thank him for it come tomorrow.

"So you'll keep the car?" Dad asked.

"I'll keep the car." I hugged them both. "Thank you."

We emptied Mother's things from the car and she patted the hood wistfully. "Take good care of her. No eating takeout on a stakeout, you hear."

I smiled at her feeble joke. "I'll bring her back when I buy my own car."

"I'll never get her back, then."

I couldn't exactly argue with that.

Dad gave some instructions about oil changes, check-ups, and what gas to put into her—which I didn't really listen, because he would remind me again, or do them himself—before letting me go. Alone in the car, I got nervous again. Trevor had been a calming and encouraging presence next to me, advising me on correct lanes and best routes. Now I didn't even seem to know the way home, as if it was different than when I was sitting in the passenger seat.

Gathering myself, I got the car moving, though my palms were a little damp and my hands kept gliding on the steering wheel before I dried them on the legs of my jeans. I drove south to 18th Avenue, where I should've turned east, but I didn't want to take Ocean Parkway with its multiple lanes, so I turned west instead. It would be a small detour through a residential area, but much quieter.

In my eagerness to find an easier route, I completely forgot that on the 18th there was a certain Irish bar that had to be avoided at all costs. Not because it was a favorite among the cops of the 70th Precinct, my brother included. Not even entirely because it was owned by Scott Brady, my cheating bastard of an ex-husband, although that was reason enough.

No, it had to be avoided because I'd made an utter ass of myself there.

I'd avoided even thinking about that Saturday two weeks ago. Or tried to avoid thinking of it. My mind kept returning to it like an addict to a fix, making me feel worse every time I recalled the incident.

It should've been simple. Go in, say hello to the bastard, ask what he'd been doing the past six years since I'd found him dipping his dick into a groupie in a back room of a concert venue and consequently divorced him.

Instead, I'd stood transfixed when he performed a song with his gravelly whiskey voice, reminiscing about the good things in our short marriage—I'm not saying it was only about sex, but my good places got all tingly—and then had stared at him tongue-tied when I finally came face to face with him. And just as I'd been about to say something, some bleached bitch with fake boobs had stuck her tongue down his throat, and he'd let her.

I have no recollection of how I got out of the bar and into Trevor's car. He'd had the good sense to follow and he'd driven me home.

He'd tried to reason with me. "You've been divorced for six years. Scott was bound to find someone new."

"I haven't found anyone. Why should he?" Although, the man had cheated on me, so it shouldn't have come as such a shock that he had. Yet I'd been barely operational.

"That's because you haven't dated in six years."

"How would I have found time for dating when I was working ten-hour shifts seven days a week?"

"Meanwhile you're twenty-seven and you aren't even trying."

"You're thirty-one. I haven't exactly seen you with a steady girlfriend."

"At least I date occasionally."

We'd wisely left it at that, but I hadn't returned to Scott's bar since—and that was another gripe. I was busting my ass off simply to pay the rent and he'd had money enough to buy a bar?

I kept my attention on traffic as I neared the bar, deliberately not looking towards it. I lucked out and the street I needed to take turned off right before it. I sighed in silent relief and slowed to give way to a car that was pulling out from the curb.

That's where my luck ended.

I glanced at the driver of the fine black SUV and my heart clenched in shock. As if I had conjured him, my bastard ex was sitting behind the wheel, and next to him was the skank who'd been checking his tonsils with her tongue. They were smiling at each other. Happily.

My first reaction—straight from my suddenly aching gut—was to hit the brakes, turn the car around and flee as fast as I could, one-way street be damned. Second reaction, probably from another organ entirely, was to accelerate and ram the side of their car. The satisfaction of imagining it felt so good that it eased the pain in my stomach.

So I did neither. I simply let them pull out.

And then I followed.

I didn't mean to. I hadn't even spied on Scott with all the resources available for me at the agency—I was really proud of my self-control, by the way—but now he was here and I had a car.

At first it was just a matter of having to drive behind them—it was a one-way street after all—but when they turned east on Lawrence Avenue, I did too. Then they took Ocean Parkway south and I didn't even hesitate getting on it, even though trying to avoid it had led me to this situation in the first place.

I barely registered the traffic. Feverish excitement and determination kept me in its hold, sharpening my mind. I had to find out where they were going. Nothing was impossible for me, not even navigating a four lane highway. I was even happy there was traffic; it allowed me to keep a car or two between ours so he wouldn't notice me.

Scott drove all the way to Avenue U, where he turned east towards Marine Park. It was a really nice neighborhood, the kind we couldn't have afforded to live in back when we were married. I'd been a twenty-year-old college dropout and he'd been a leader of a band that never made it. We hadn't even had a permanent home. His band was on tour the whole time we were married, and I'd followed them. I wasn't entirely sure a tame middle-class neighborhood like this would've even been our style.

It still wasn't my style, but I guess he'd changed.

He drove to the northeastern corner of the park from which the neighborhood got its name, a large area of saltwater marsh and recreational spaces that stretched all the way to Jamaica Bay, before turning north on 38th Street.

One side of the road was redbrick row-houses, nice and neat, and the other was semis with different façades on every half. He drove into the tiny driveway of one of the larger semis; their half was pink and the other half light blue. I didn't slow down but continued on before pulling over a couple of houses up between two cars that would hide mine.

I aced the parallel parking this time round. Nothing was impossible for me in my current state.

I watched from the side mirror as Scott and that woman exited the car and took groceries from the trunk. He looked good in low-riding jeans and a T; she looked skanky in tight shorts and a spaghetti-strap top that barely contained her assets, her long blond hair in a ponytail. Laughing at some joke, they went into the house.

The moment they disappeared, the spell that had kept me going released. I looked around, bewildered, not believing what I'd done. I'd actually followed my ex-husband across half of Brooklyn. Had I really turned into that woman?

Angry with myself, and hugely embarrassed, I was about to drive home, never to return, when someone knocked on my side window. I shrieked and put a hand in my pocket to dig out my pepper spray—that wasn't there—but then Jackson peeked in.

"Tracy? What the hell are you doing here?"

It took a moment for my heart to stop thumping out of my chest. I lowered the window. "Cruising?"

"Outside my house?"

"You live here?"

I took a proper look at my surroundings. I was outside a semi that was half white shingles and half really nice grayish-blue clapboard, both sides in good repair. The tiny front yard between the houses was half expertly landscaped garden—the white side—and half dried grass. Jackson's car was parked on the short driveway next to the barren patch.

"Let me guess, the blue half is yours?"

"Are you saying you didn't Google my address the first chance you got?" he asked amused. I had Googled it, actually, with the street view even. I just hadn't paid attention to where I was driving.

"Out with it. Why are you here?"

"I was trailing a car."

"Whose car? And where did you get this car?"

I decided to go with the latter question first. "It's my mom's. She and Dad insisted I take it."

"Pretty. Cheryl will be green with envy."

"I know," I said, smiling. Cheryl loved all things pink, but a cherry red car had to come a close second. Even I loved the color and I wasn't terribly into reds.

Jackson opened the door for me and I got out. "Let's have a cup of coffee and you can tell me all about it."

Chapter Six

I FOLLOWED JACKSON INTO HIS HOUSE and looked around, shamelessly curious. A small hall opened onto a living room-dining room combo to the left—although the dining room appeared to be his home office—and a kitchen at the back of the hallway. Narrow stairs led upstairs. Judging by the size of the downstairs, I presumed there would be two or three small bedrooms and a bath there.

The place was done in muted tones, brown leather and wood; the old-fashioned wallpapers were rather faded, and the hardwood floors could've used a new coat of varnish—and a good vacuuming. The furniture was less eclectic than my 70s collection from the Salvation Army thrift store, and much older, but they were oak or some other hardwood that had aged well. Only the leather recliner and the large TV were modern.

"This is nothing like I expected."

"I inherited this from my uncle, like I did the agency."

He pointed at a photo on the hallway wall of a man in his late fifties who was portly, balding, and wearing a brown suit and a trench coat. The only thing missing was a fedora. Then he'd have looked exactly like I thought a P.I. should. Jackson had initially been a bit of a disappointment in that respect, but I'd got over it and now thought that his uniform of black jeans, black T-shirt and black sneakers with a black blazer was exactly how a P.I. should look.

According to Trevor, Jackson had quit the police force four years ago because his partner had been killed during a murder investigation. Jackson hadn't spoken about that, but had told me that his uncle, who had started the agency, had died childless and had left the agency to him. But I wasn't ready to discard Trevor's version either. My boss had hidden depths he wouldn't reveal easily.

"It's very ... manly."

Jackson grinned as he led me into the kitchen. "I've had no reason to redecorate." The kitchen attested to that with its old-fashioned cupboards and linoleum floor. Only the appliances were new.

He poured us large mugs of coffee he had ready and we went to the back porch to enjoy the day, sitting on old wicker chairs that he'd likely inherited with the rest of the furniture, judging by the squeaks and groans they made under us.

The back yard wasn't much larger than the front, and was equally barren, with only a tool shed at the back that I'd wager didn't contain any gardening tools. It might have held a large grill.

I could imagine him having friends over for a barbeque.

Then again, I'd never met any of his friends, if you didn't count his old colleagues from his homicide detective days. And I knew nothing of his family, other than that his childhood hadn't been nice. But he'd had the uncle, so maybe there were other relatives he could invite over.

I liked that image.

Tall fences separated the yard from the neighbors', but I could see from the porch that both had those huge round fiberglass pools that were easy to install. They took up pretty much the entire adjoining lawns, but there was still at least some vegetation. Jackson barely had grass growing in his.

"This looks easy to maintain."

"I'm not exactly a gardener. Now, are you ready to talk?"

I groaned. "It's embarrassing."

"More embarrassing than falling into a dumpster?"

"Infinitely."

"This should be good, then."

I sighed. "I was driving home from my parents' when I spotted my scumbag of an ex's car, and the next thing I know I'm parked outside your house."

Jackson tried so hard not to smile that an honest-to-God dimple that I'd never seen before appeared on his cheek. Then his better side lost the battle and he burst out laughing.

"He really did a number on you, didn't he?" he asked when he finally could talk again, wiping his eyes.

I nodded, miserable. "The worst thing is, I thought I was over him. But I simply haven't dealt with it at all." I'd buried myself so deep in work I'd been too busy to think about my failed marriage. No wonder I hadn't been interested in dating.

"I'm not exactly the best person to have this kind of talk with, you know."

"Tough. You're the only person I got."

I startled when I realized it was the truth. I used to have a close girlfriend, Jessica, my old roommate, but since she'd moved in with her boyfriend I hadn't even spoken to her. And when I was waitressing there were always women I worked with that I could share my worries with, but now I only had Jackson. And Cheryl of course, but it wasn't often I had a chance to sit down with her and gossip.

We drank our coffees in silence for a few moments.

"You knew he lived next to you?"

He didn't ask who. "Of course."

I struggled with myself and lost. "So who is she?"

"His wife."

My entire being tightened in shock until I felt like I would snap in two. I wanted to throw up.

His wife? Why hadn't I come to think of that? The blood coursing in my ears was so loud I barely heard when Jackson continued.

"Her name is Nicole, and she's thirty-one. They've been married for a year and a half. The house and the bar were her father's and she inherited them when he died."

That finally caught my attention. "So he married money?" That was so much better than if he'd actually achieved something himself. "I could totally do that."

"Where would you find a rich guy?"

"That's the tricky part. But if I found one, I could."

He lifted his coffee mug. "I'll drink to that."

I toasted back.

"They arrested Larry Williams," I said, purposely changing the topic.

"I know. Blair called me."

It took me a moment to figure out who he was talking about. Detective Kelley was such a formidable figure I didn't dare to use her first name, even in my thoughts.

"What will you tell his wife?"

"I already called her and told her we need to meet. The police didn't tell her anything when they arrested him."

"Today?"

"Yep. I don't usually do house calls on weekends, but I thought it best to make an exception." He glanced at his wristwatch. "In fact, I have to get going."

"Can I come too?"

"Absolutely. We can even take your car," he said with a smile.

"It's a great car," I defended my vehicle.

"And such a brilliant color."

We exited his house and headed to my car. My mind was occupied by Mrs. Williams—the first? the second?—and so I didn't notice the danger until it was too late.

"Tracy!"

I swiveled towards the voice hailing me, and although I hadn't expected to run into the bastard, I managed to keep my cool.

Yay me!

Scott was still dressed in the faded, low-riding jeans and T-shirt that hugged his delicious torso. His dark blond hair was a sexy mess, but I totally didn't drool. My mouth was too dry for that.

"Scott. What brings you here?"

I didn't even squeak.

"I live here." He waved his hand in the general direction of his house. Then he cast a curious look at Jackson, who was holding the door of my car open for me. "And you? Do you live here?"

"No. I came here to meet my..." An overwhelming urge seized me to claim that Jackson was my boyfriend, just to see the look on Scott's face, but I managed to hold my tongue. Although, if Jackson hadn't been here, all bets would've been off.

"Boss," I said instead.

"You work for Dean?"

"Yes. I'm a private detective," I added, just in case he thought I was his housekeeper or something.

"That's great." He sounded like he meant it, but I shrugged like it wasn't a big deal.

"Beats waiting tables."

He flushed lightly. "I own the bar."

I blinked, baffled. "Good for you. But I actually meant I was waiting tables before I became a P.I." Very recently, but I hoped he wouldn't ask any details.

"Ah. So how've you been?"

"Good. You?"

"Good."

We looked around, seeking inspiration—or a fast escape. "I hear you got married," I managed to say.

"Yeah." He glanced towards his house as if checking if he was being caught. "Her name's Nicole. She's great. What about you?"

"I've been too busy."

"Right. Crime never sleeps."

Or waitresses.

"So where did you disappear the other night?"

So he had noticed from his smooching.

"I ... got a phone call I had to take outside. It was

very loud in the bar," I added unnecessarily.

"Sure, sure." He looked as uncomfortable as I felt. "Well, it was nice running into you. Maybe we can do it again at a better time?"

"Sure," I said, and got in the car before I blew the whole thing. Jackson rounded the car to the passenger seat. "Don't say a word," I told him as I started the engine.

"I wasn't going to." But the whole drive he shook in barely controlled mirth.

Chapter Seven

LARRY AND HANNAH WILLIAMS lived in Bushwick, the northernmost neighborhood of Brooklyn before Queens, so I got to drive through the entire borough—as if I hadn't done enough driving already for one day. Hope Gardens was a massive housing project from the 80s that spanned an entire large block, with a green area in the middle—not that it was currently very well maintained. Their apartment was in the tallest, fourteen-story building, with a view towards the park and over much of the area.

Jackson and I sat side by side on a faded leather couch in their living room, feeling acutely uncomfortable. I was, anyway. It was difficult to tell how Jackson was feeling; he had retreated behind his professional mask. My current life goal was to be able to do the same, but for now I had to settle with the myriad of smiles I'd developed during my six years as a waitress. I had one for every occasion, and they hid my true feelings pretty well too. But I couldn't smile here.

"We can only give you the facts that we have," Jackson told Mrs. Williams, who was sitting opposite us.

She was in her early forties and would probably have been pretty if her eyes hadn't been puffed up from crying. She'd been crying when we came, nothing to do with us. She was tall—much taller than her husband—and large—not fat, but big boned. Sheila had been delicately built and short, so it seemed Larry Williams had an eclectic taste in women.

"I'm afraid your husband was being unfaithful," he continued. I admired how he formulated it. It gave the truth but not the whole truth. We'd agreed that until we knew for sure, we wouldn't reveal the bigamy to Mrs. Williams. It would make her upset—more upset.

Mrs. Williams sobbed. "I knew it. He was always away from home at the oddest times. He claimed he was at the racetrack but I didn't believe it." She wiped her eyes with the back of her hand. "Who is she?"

"Unfortunately, we haven't got that far in our investigation yet. We just wanted to give you an update in the light of today's events."

We actually knew the name of the woman Larry Williams had spent the night with—Carol Marr—but Jackson didn't want us to divulge it either, as it might hinder the murder investigation.

"I just don't understand why they arrested him. Larry wouldn't hurt a fly, and they told me he … he killed a woman."

"At the moment he's a person of interest. We'll know

more when the coroner has the time of death determined."

"So there is a dead woman?" She looked slightly green.

"Yes."

"The one he was…" She couldn't finish the sentence.

"She wasn't the woman he spent last night with, as far as we know, but we can't rule out at this point that he was having an affair with the dead woman as well."

Since he and Sheila were married, I'd say he was definitely having an affair with her.

Mrs. Williams went completely still. "He had more than one woman?"

I understood the shock and pain in her voice. I'd only caught Scott doing that one groupie, but who knew how many of them he'd had behind my back. Women had been throwing themselves at him everywhere the band played.

"Should I bring you a glass of water?" I asked, worried when she went alarmingly white underneath all the puffy red. She nodded and I shot up and headed to the small kitchenette. It was clean and sparsely furnished, like the entire apartment, only the bare necessities in every room. Cupboards were almost empty too, as I noticed when I was trying to find a glass. No staples there even. Who didn't have at least coffee in their cupboard?

When I returned with the water I checked the photos

on the living room wall. Family and friends in them, as you'd expect. And there was their wedding photo too, taken, if I wasn't very much mistaken, in Las Vegas.

I gave the glass to Mrs. Williams, who held it with both hands so it wouldn't shake. I sat back down, trying to come up with a way to bring up their marriage. In the end I went with the direct approach.

"Have you been married long?"

"Four years. You'd think a man could remain faithful for four measly years." Mine couldn't remain faithful for a year, but I kept that to myself. "We met in Vegas and it was love at first sight. So romantic. We were married by the end of the week." She sighed. "Perhaps it was too hasty. But our troubles didn't start until we moved here a couple of years ago. We lived in Vegas at first."

"You're not from around here?"

"I'm not. But I don't have any family and Larry wanted to be closer to his, so we moved here. It was very exciting at first, but then I couldn't find a job. It's not fun being all alone in a strange city without a job."

"Does Larry have a job?"

"Nothing permanent."

We left soon thereafter. I kept my questions to myself until we were back at my car. Jackson wanted to drive, and since I was pretty tired of all the driving I'd already done that day, I let him.

"Are you expensive?"

"What?" His startled look made me smile.

"Your fees. You can pretty much choose your clients, can't you?"

"Yes."

"And the kind of surveillance we did for Mrs. Williams, hours of it, is extra expensive, isn't it?" He nodded and I continued: "So how can Mrs. Williams afford it? She's unemployed and lives in a project. Her cupboards were empty. Even if she were on food stamps there'd be something in them."

Jackson nodded, contemplating. "Good point. She paid the advance promptly and didn't even try to haggle."

"I think that's very odd."

"We're not being paid to investigate Mrs. Williams's finances," Jackson said sternly.

"Couldn't we at least take a peek?"

"No."

"Then how about finding out how it was possible for Larry Williams to marry two women?"

"If the marriages were registered in different states, it could be no one noticed. Especially since one of the marriages was held in the Chapel of Love."

"So you saw the photo too?"

"I did."

We dropped the topic, but I couldn't shake the feeling there was something odd about the situation.

Jarod was watching TV and eating Chinese takeout on the sofa when I got home after a detour to Jackson's to leave him off. The scent of his food made my stomach growl, and I realized I hadn't had anything but coffee since lunch. I plopped next to him and pilfered a spring roll.

"Did you have a good day?"

"Yeah. Cyber threat avoided."

"You don't look happy." He looked miserable, actually.

"Term starts tomorrow."

"That's good, isn't it?"

"No."

"You're not bullied, are you?" I asked, worried. For all that he was a genius he was slightly clueless about life in general. Plus, everyone in his post grad class was older than him. He'd graduated from college at the age most people started it.

"No."

Then the real reason for his misery hit me. "You're afraid you'll run into your ex-girlfriend, aren't you?" He'd broken up with her at the start of the summer when she accused him of spending more time with his computers than her. Then she'd smashed said computers with a baseball bat.

"Bound to," he said, crestfallen.

"I ran into my ex-husband today and survived it."

"Yeah? My girlfriend is dating the captain of the college football team now. I'm pretty sure I wouldn't survive an encounter with him."

I had to laugh. "My ex is now married to a long-legged blonde with fake—I hope—boobs who gave him a bar to run."

That elicited a smile from him. "You win."

"I totally do." I jumped up, as full of energy as I'd been without a moment earlier. "Come on, the mall's still open and I have a car. Let's go buy you school stuff. That'll cheer you up."

We ended up having a good time at the mall, and when we got home we stayed up later than either of us had meant to. When my alarm woke me up at six the next morning I almost threw it against the wall. But I'd set the time myself, so after a few moments of self-pity I forced myself up. The next step took considerably more willpower: putting on my new jogging gear.

Jarod hadn't been the only one shopping last evening. Of all places, I'd ended up in a sportswear store. I blamed it on the weird day I'd had. It had absolutely nothing do with wanting to be in great shape the next time I ran into Scott.

Absolutely nothing.

The salesperson at the store had spotted an easy mark and had tried to sell me everything I might need and half the things I didn't, and all of it with the highest price possible. I'd stayed firm and bought only what I needed. Still, he had somehow managed to sell me tight, knee-length spandex—or Lycra or whatever—shorts that took a lot of tucking and rolling of my hips to pull over my bottom. They squished my flesh nice and tight, but the result was so unnerving that I rummaged through my closet for an old pair of cut-off sweat shorts to wear over them. The purple spandex—or whatever—tank-top got to stay though. I looked great in it, if I could say so myself. It squeezed my boobs and managed to hide the tummy rolls. Well, most of them anyway.

The running shoes were turquoise and felt unlike anything I'd ever worn, definitely nothing like the last pair I'd bought in high school. They were light and breathable and felt almost like I had nothing in my feet. Even if I only went running this one time, I was keeping the shoes.

I tiptoed out of the apartment and took the stairs down as an expression of my new, sportier life. I pushed the front door open and stepped briskly out.

The early morning air hit me so hard it cut my breath short. I was instantly freezing in my tank-top and shorts. Perhaps I should've worn a sweatshirt after all. But I wouldn't go back for it or I'd never leave my home again. I dashed to my car and put the heater on at full blast. Fifteen minutes later I was banging at Jackson's door.

Chapter Eight

"RISE AND SHINE," I SANG when Jackson finally opened the door. It took him so long I'd begun to freeze again, but I didn't let that mar my good mood.

"Tracy? What the fuck?" He looked like I'd managed to wake him up, rumpled, bleary-eyed, and kind of confused. Pretty cute, actually. He was wearing boxer briefs—I looked, so sue me—and had a sweatshirt on backwards, so he must have pulled it on in haste.

His legs looked every bit as fine as I'd always thought they would, by the way, lean and strong.

"I'm starting a new life and I'll be damned if I do it alone. So put on your running gear and take me to the park."

"At..." He glanced at his wristwatch. "Six-thirty in the morning? Are you insane?"

Having managed to pull the reverse of my nightmare, I beamed at him. "If I don't do it early, I'll never do it."

"This is somehow my fault, isn't it?" he asked, rubbing his face with both hands, which only managed to make him look more bleary-eyed. I'd never seen my boss so out of balance before.

"Sure is. You shouldn't have given me those condemning glances whenever you spoke of running."

Since he couldn't deny he'd done that, he retreated to the foyer and disappeared upstairs. Five minutes later we were out the door—men could dress up really fast when they had to—and heading on foot to Marine Park that started right at the southern end of his street.

"You're not wearing spandex," I observed when we reached the park and the path that started at the corner there. He had opted for more traditional light grey sweatpants and a cotton T-shirt—white, to my surprise. I wouldn't have thought he owned shirts in other color than black. His running shoes were similar to mine though, but well-used. He must run often.

"Or whatever this material is," I added, tugging my shirt.

"God forbid."

"Pity. Look how nice that guy's abs look in it."

And the back view was even better, I noticed, after he'd passed us, the tight shorts giving him a nice butt-lift. Or it could be his muscles were actually that tight. Maybe there was something to be said for jogging after all. And definitely for spandex. Or whatever.

Jackson only huffed. "Have you done any exercising lately?"

"Define lately."

"O-kay…"

He started to run, setting a pace that was easy for me to keep up with, despite the fact that his legs were much longer than mine. But I managed maybe five hundred yards before I had to cry for a pause. Black spots were dancing in my eyes and I leaned my hands against my knees, but he wouldn't let me stop.

"Keep walking until you can breathe again."

I groaned but obeyed. Another five hundred yards later he began to run again, and I followed. We kept alternating between walking and running, although the running bits were getting shorter and my groaning louder whenever I had to switch from walking. With me bitching the entire time, threatening to do bad things to him the moment I caught my breath, we rounded the park—or the shortest path there.

"Okay, great start," he told me when we reached the corner of the park where we'd started from, smiling, as if I hadn't made the exercise a hell on Earth for him. "Tomorrow we'll do this again."

"Nooooo…"

"Do I have to come and fetch you?" he asked sternly. Now that I'd opened this particular Pandora's Box, there clearly was no closing it. But I was sorely regretting my initiative already. Not even spandex made the exercising fun.

Fine, *Lycra*.

Having him fetch me would be too much like in my nightmare, so I shook my head. "I'll be there."

"But maybe after seven?" I agreed to that, willingly. "Now, since I'm here, I think I'll run a few rounds more. You can find the way back to the car?" He pointed towards his street.

"Of course." I waited until he had disappeared around a bend—running three times faster than with me—before limping to my car.

Jonny Moreira was leaning against it.

My determined limping didn't falter I'm proud to say. It should've though, because he was intimidating. He was in his early thirties and six-foot-three of looming muscle. His shoulders were almost too wide for his tailor-made suit jacket; his black hair was combed back and his dark eyes were set deep in an angular face. He looked like a mafia goon, which in itself wasn't a reason to be wary of him.

That he actually was a henchman to a New Jersey drug lord who'd recently set shop in Brooklyn, however, was.

"Did you have a good run?" he asked with a hint of a smile, straightening up when I reached him. He had a deep voice and a slight Jersey accent.

"How do you know I've been out running?" When he gave a meaningful—and a tad too interested—look at my outfit, I amended: "How did you know I'd be running here?"

"I followed you from your home."

The matter of fact statement froze me. "I didn't notice you."

"I'm good."

"Right..." He actually was though. This wasn't the first time he'd managed to follow me without me being any wiser. "Then why didn't you talk to me there?"

"You were too busy getting into your car. I wasn't fast enough."

"It was cold."

That made him smile. "I didn't take you for a runner." Since he'd actually witnessed me chasing after a fugitive, he made a solid point.

"I wasn't. But then I learned that my ex-husband is married to a Barbie doll." I don't know why I confessed him that.

He snorted a laugh. "That would do it. Get in the car, we need to talk."

"I'm not getting into a car with you ever again." The last time I'd been held at gunpoint. Not a fond memory.

He shook his head, exasperated. "You'll freeze to death in that outfit. Get in the car. I'll stand out here."

That sounded better, and since I was actually getting cold—the morning hadn't warmed yet and I was sweaty—I did so. I lowered the window.

"What do you want?"

He leaned against the hood, idly scanning the street for threats. He likely couldn't help it.

"I want to know who killed Sheila Rinaldi."

"What?"

He gave me a calm look. "I've seen the police report. You were there."

"With the risk of repeating myself … what? How?"

"I have my sources."

"There are more crooked cops than Lonnie Peters?"

Lonnie had actually been fired when it turned out he'd been working for Craig Douglas, and the previous drug lord too. He was awaiting trial.

He huffed. "He was nothing." I didn't like the sound of that.

"Well, if you've seen the reports you know more than I do. I only found the body."

"You were in her apartment. What was in there?"

His voice was really intense, so I frowned, curious. "Why do you want to know?"

"She was my cousin."

I pulled back in surprise. "I'm sorry for your loss," I said automatically.

"Sorry doesn't bring me her murderer." His dark brows furrowed in sorrow and anger.

"Can't you just let the police do their job?"

"I don't trust the police."

"Not all of them are in the pocket of the mafia."

"I'm not in the mafia," he said, exasperated.

"You could have fooled me."

"Craig Douglas is a legitimate businessman."

"Who just buys cops for fun?"

"Lonnie Peters was MacRath's man. We just took advantage of him."

"Right..."

"Will you help me or what?"

"I don't know what you think I can do that the police can't. And it's my brother in charge of the investigation. He's good."

Moreira growled. "Was it her husband who killed her?"

"Larry Williams?"

"How many husbands do you think she had?"

"I don't know. But Larry definitely had more than one wife."

He pressed his fists against the hood and pushed with such angry force I feared he'd dent it.

"I'll kill him."

"There's no killing of anyone if you want me to help you."

"Was. It. Him?"

"No."

He pulled back. "Just like that? Even though the police have him in custody?"

"We have his whereabouts for most of the night, but it's more a gut feeling," I confessed. "Couldn't it have been one of your people?"

"My people?"

"You know, mafia. Isn't yours a family business?"

"I'm not in the mafia, for fuck's sake."

"You're not exactly a Boy Scout either. You're a drug dealer." And I'd do well to remember it. "Maybe you have an uncle or a cousin who got her involved in something she shouldn't have and this was payback?"

Moreira pinched the bridge of his nose, curbing his anger. "Sheila was a good girl. She worked at the Aqueduct Racetrack booking office and didn't have so much as a speeding ticket."

"Is that where she met Larry?"

"What?"

"His wife—the other wife who hired us in the first place—told us he liked to go to the racetrack, but she didn't believe him."

"I don't know how they met."

"How long had they been married?"

"Six months or so."

"Was there anyone significant before Larry?"

"Why, you think the previous guy would've killed her? After all this time?"

"I've been divorced for six years and I still want to kill my ex. Although I'd much rather kill his current wife."

A smile ghosted on his lips. "I guess it's worth checking out. I'll let you know."

He turned to leave, but paused and then straightened to his full height. I reached my head out of the car window to see what kind of threat he had spotted and all but hit my head in my haste to pull back. Scott. He was in a bathrobe that gave me a glimpse of his sculpted chest, and wearing slippers, and his hair was messier than ever. He looked good enough to eat.

"Is everything all right, Tracy?" His voice was full of concern and he ignored Moreira completely. Impressive and foolish.

"Of course," I snapped, annoyed both for his interruption and my reaction to him. "Why wouldn't it be?"

"I thought maybe he wouldn't let you leave." He nodded towards Moreira, straightening and assessing him. Moreira just smiled.

"We were having a chat. And he may be big, but even he can't win against a car. If I wanted to leave, I would've."

"You two know each other?"

"Yes, we do. He's my..." And again the urge to flaunt a nonexistent boyfriend before Scott was almost a physical force. But I rallied. "Client," I managed to say. "And this is a private conversation, if you don't mind."

Scott shot a searching glance at me, and then

Moreira, who had resumed his calm pose against my car. "Okay. Yell if you need help," he said, as he turned to leave.

I made a face at his retreating back. "You're the last person I'll need for anything," I muttered.

"Let me guess. The ex-husband?" Moreira asked, amused.

"Yes."

"I'd want to kill him too if I were you."

"There'll be no killing of anyone." But he just grinned and turned to head to his car. "Thanks for the lockpicks," I shouted after him, and he lifted his hand in acknowledgement.

Chapter Nine

AFTER THE ENCOUNTER WITH Moreira, I couldn't just leave, so I settled down to wait. Jackson returned a few minutes later, jogging at a steady pace, but he almost tripped in surprise when he saw me on his porch.

"What are you still doing here?" He went past me to open his front door. He wasn't even winded after his run, the showoff. I made to follow him in.

"Moreira was waiting for me."

That made him pause on the threshold, blocking my way so suddenly I almost bumped into him. "Ah. I'd hoped he'd left by then."

"You knew he was there?"

"Yes."

"And didn't tell me?" I asked incredulous. The two of them didn't exactly see eye to eye, and I would've thought he'd warn me.

"I thought you knew."

"Well, I didn't. But never mind that." I waved my hand dismissively to get back to business. "We need to talk."

He cocked a brow. "Is it the kind of talk that can't

wait until I've showered and maybe had some breakfast?"

Since I desperately needed both myself, I shook my head. "I guess we can talk at the office."

"Excellent. See you there." And he disappeared through his door.

"Nice abs," I yelled after him, having spied them through the sweaty T-shirt that hugged his stomach. In a considerably better mood, I got into my car and drove home.

After the shower and breakfast I'd regained enough energy to tackle Jarod out of bed. I'd never had to wake him up before—he seemed to get by with a minimum of sleep—but the first day of the term turned out to be different. I couldn't really blame him. The mere thought of returning to college, like my family wanted me to, was enough to break me out in hives.

"I don't want to go," he groaned as I pulled him up by his arms.

"Tough. Now put on your nice new clothes, comb your hair, and get going." If I sounded like my mother, I couldn't help it. It took some more coaxing and an extra-large mug of coffee, but I managed to push him out of the door in time.

Wiping my brow, I was leaning against the closed door, catching—figuratively—my breath, when an envelope was pushed underneath it. I stared baffled at the white rectangle at my feet for so long that when I finally thought to check who had delivered it, the hallway was empty.

I picked up the envelope and opened it. I read the contents, and my entire being froze and then boiled up. I read it again, getting even angrier on the second go. Furious now, and in desperate need of a clearer head, I called my brother Travis.

Travis was the oldest of the four of us, eight years older than me. He was the most successful of us too, or would be once he got his political career going. For now he was a defense attorney at the Brooklyn Defender Service, helping criminals without means. He wasn't a philanthropist by nature, but he'd married rich, so he could afford it and still have the lifestyle of a business lawyer. Plus, it would look good in his resume when he entered into politics.

"Are you busy?"

"I'm always busy, you know that," he said slightly irritated.

"But can you talk?"

"Yes, I'm at the office." It was only a little past eight, but I wasn't surprised. On top of being overworked he had four-year-old twin boys at home. I'd spend as much time at work as possible too if I had to live with Damiens 1 and 2.

"What's up?"

"My landlord just sent me a notice that the rent will go up by five hundred dollars." Saying it aloud made my blood pressure rise.

"That's excessive."

"And also, you know, illegal. This is a rent stabilized apartment."

"Did he give you a reason?"

"Yes. Because there's a new tenant in the apartment the old lease isn't valid anymore. But this is my apartment. The lease is in my name. Aren't I allowed to decide who lives here?"

He sighed. "I'll look into it, though this isn't exactly my area of expertise. Can you get the notice and your current lease for me?"

"I can drop them on my way to work."

Driving in the Monday morning rush was a less pleasant experience than cruising on the Sunday-empty streets. It didn't help that I was seething already when I got in the car. I was yelling profanities and making rude hand gestures before I was past Prospect Park, and my shoulders were so stiff from angrily squeezing the steering wheel I feared I'd lose blood flow to my brain.

Brooklyn Defender Services was in Downtown, on the seventh floor of an ordinary office building. Parking was in a multi-story garage across the street, so I didn't have to stress about that, although the line into the garage at that time of morning was staggering.

It wasn't yet nine when I arrived at the Defender Services' offices and found the doors locked. I called Travis, and a moment later a secretary in her early forties came to let me in. She gave me a curious look, took in my jeans and T-shirt, and all but rolled her eyes. She did roll her eyes when she checked my P.I. ID. I got the notion that my showing up hadn't improved Travis's standing in the office.

I hadn't been here before and I studied the place curious when I followed the woman to Travis's office at the other end of a long hallway. It was bland—beige walls and vomit color carpets—and Travis's office was small—and bland. This was a government agency, after all. What space there was in his room was crammed with bookshelves full of ring binders and law books. It was impossible to see the top of his desk for all the papers on it.

"I guess you weren't kidding when you said you're overworked," I said dryly when the secretary had left us, getting in.

He rounded his desk to come and give me a hug. He was tall, with a lean, athletic body—he'd put himself through college with a varsity scholarship—and Dad's looks and dark coloring—well, before Dad went gray. He took himself a bit too seriously for my tastes, and the age difference had ensured we weren't terribly close, but he was my brother and I knew he'd stand up for me.

"I only have a moment before my first client shows up."

"I don't need long. Here are the documents." I handed him the papers and he gave them a cursory look. "Do you think you can make him change his mind?"

"I can't say until I've looked these through."

"Just don't lose them in all this," I said in mock horror, waving at his desk, and he smiled.

"I have a system."

His intercom beeped and the secretary spoke: "A Mrs. Williams for you."

I perked. "Hannah Williams?" Williams was a common name, but surely they wouldn't all need legal assistance at the same time.

Travis checked his appointment book. "Yes. Do you know her?"

"She's our client. Or was, until her husband we were hired to track was arrested for murder yesterday. And possibly for bigamy too. But she doesn't know about the latter yet," I added hastily, "so don't tell her."

Travis frowned and then pressed the intercom button. "Five minutes," he said to his secretary. And then back to me: "Talk."

I gave him as concise a version as I could of what had happened the previous day. I left out the unfortunate incident with the dumpster though—to save time, naturally—even if Travis could probably have used a good laugh. He listened attentively and only asked questions when I'd finished.

"So the victim is the second, bigamous wife?"

"Yes."

"But it's not certain the husband did it?"

"I don't know the time of death yet, so I can't say for sure."

"No one knows yet. This isn't TV. Educated guess?"

That he valued my opinion made my chest swell in pride. I gave it a thought. "The rug in the victim's house was still wet with blood. I think she was killed early that morning, and for that time we have his whereabouts covered."

"I'll look into it should I take up his defense. Maybe I'll get him freed on that."

"There's still the bigamy to consider."

He sneered, full of lawyerly arrogance. "I'm being hired for the murder case." Meaning, he didn't have to care about the bigamy.

"In that case, would you consider hiring us as investigators?" Technically, Moreira had asked first, but we'd have better access to everything as part of the official investigation. He wouldn't mind.

"I'll think about it. Now, you'll have to go or I'll be late the whole day. This client was already extra. Oh, and take the corridor to the right. No need for you to come face to face with Mrs. Williams at this point." I did as told and managed to get out without running into our erstwhile client.

It took twenty minutes to cover the ten minute drive to the agency—I now officially hated driving in morning traffic, by the way—plus ten minutes to find a parking spot—I ended up to the garage two blocks from the agency Jackson and Cheryl used. So it was already almost ten before I entered the small reception area of Jackson Dean Investigations on the second floor of a low redbrick building at the corner of Flatbush Avenue and Bergen Street.

I was greeted with the delighted barking of Misty Morning, Cheryl's border terrier Yorkie mix that followed her everywhere. She was wearing a pretty pink coat and a bow on her head, and kept jumping against my legs until I picked her up. She instantly tried to lick my face.

"Where have you been?" Cheryl asked from behind her desk. She was in her early fifties with blond bouffant hair, a heavily made-up face, and a tendency to dress in pink clothes a size too small for her round figure.

"I had to visit my brother Travis."

The door to Jackson's office was thrown open with a loud bang and he stood in the doorway, looking thunderous. "I'd think that if you had such important news for me that you forewent breakfast and shower for it, you'd have the courtesy of showing up at work on time."

He had a bit of a temper at times, but he cooled down fast too, so I ignored his mood. "There's been a development."

"This had better be good."

He marched back to his desk and I exchanged a commiserating look with Cheryl. "What's this about shower and breakfast," she asked, shamelessly curious, almost making me blush—though what there was to blush about, I couldn't say.

"We went for a jog together," I said lightly, following Jackson in, Misty at my heels. She often sat next to me on the comfy couch in Jackson's office, my official work space. I'd managed to gather enough papers, books, and files on the coffee table in front of it over the past three weeks to make the table overflow.

I guess Travis and I weren't so different after all.

The table barely had room for the coffee mug that was currently perched on one corner. I was wondering if I had time to take it to the other side of the room where the coffee maker stood and fill it with fresh goodness, but one look at Jackson's face made me take a seat instead.

"Talk."

"What is it with men and their need to give curt orders?" But he wasn't easily amused this morning, so I sighed and got on with it. "I dropped by Travis' offices this morning. The reason I was late, by the way. Mrs.

Williams just hired him to defend her husband in the murder case, and if he's able he'll hire us on it."

He blinked. "And you know this because?"

"She showed up at his offices when I was there."

He contemplated my news with a frown. "Did she see you?"

"No."

He nodded. "And what did Moreira want?"

"That we find out who killed Sheila Rinaldi."

"What?" He looked as flabbergasted as I'd felt at the time.

"My reaction exactly. Turns out they were cousins."

He stared at me for a few heartbeats, then he gave a longsuffering sigh. "You'd best tell me everything."

Chapter Ten

ALF AN HOUR LATER WE were in Jackson's car, driving towards Ozone Park in southern Queens and the Aqueduct Racetrack there. Travis had called before I'd finished my account to Jackson and given us the green light to investigate the murder.

"Until we have the time of death, they'll consider my client the prime suspect for the murder and won't look for others, so it's in our best interest you find the killer."

And the best place to start was to find out everything about Sheila Rinaldi, who had worked at the racetrack.

"Should I have told Travis that Moreira wants us to investigate too?"

His name made Jackson frown. "It's not like he hired us officially."

"So it's not a conflict of interest or whatever?"

"No."

"He promised to find out if Sheila had a steady boyfriend before Larry who might have wanted to kill her."

Jackson's frown deepened. If I didn't know better, I'd say he didn't like Moreira. Then again, he had held the man at gunpoint, so it was probably exactly the case.

"Good," he only said though.

"I suggested she might have become involved in some mafia stuff, but he insisted he's not in the mafia."

Jackson sneered, but let that go too. "There are other ways to get in trouble at the racetrack. Maybe she placed bets she shouldn't have and owed money, or was blackmailed into fixing bets." Then he sighed. "But the boyfriend is a better call. It takes great personal emotion to kill someone by bashing their head in."

"That's what Trevor said." I tried and failed not to imagine that kind of rage. "Maybe her ex found out that she'd married, or something, and got angry." Maybe he was in mafia too, no matter what Moreira tried to claim to the contrary.

"I'd still put my money on Larry Williams."

"I just can't imagine him bashing anyone's head in."

"There is that."

"Moreira asked what was in the apartment," I said, thinking back at the place, "but there wasn't anything, was there?"

"Not that I noticed, but we were there for such a short time."

"But there weren't even signs of a struggle."

He spared a glance at me from the traffic and nodded. "You're right."

"So what does that mean?"

"We'd better find out."

I'd never been to the Aqueduct Racetrack before—no one gambled in our house, and definitely not on ponies—and I didn't know what to expect. The sheer size of the place hit me first. We approached the compound from the west, where the clubhouse and stand were, but even though they were huge—the seats for over ten thousand spectators were on one side of the track only—they weren't large enough to cover the length of the track itself. Parking lots circled the track on three sides and went on for miles. Seemed like, anyway.

"Not many cars here," I noted as Jackson drove to the main admission gate.

"The season won't start until November."

"You're a betting man?"

I asked it lightly, but the bitter twist of Jackson's lips suggested I'd hit a nerve.

"My father was." Since he'd once revealed he'd had the kind of childhood where he much preferred to hang out in his friends' houses—mine included—than home, I let it be.

We were directed from the admission gate to the employee entrance at the south end of the clubhouse. The parking lot there was pretty full. "So what are these people here for, then, if the season's not started?"

"This is a casino too, and there are restaurants."

A security guard at the entrance checked our

credentials before directing us to the employee manager's office on the first floor. Emily Hunter was in her late thirties, with a honey-color shoulder-length hair, and dressed for a PR job in a pinstripe skirt suit and black Louboutin pumps—yes, I know what they look like—instead of a job in an office where no one could see her. She gave Jackson an appreciating look, which he didn't notice—the idiot—and ignored me completely. I was fine with that.

"What can I do for you, Mr. Dean?" she all but purred, but Jackson had retreated behind his work mask and didn't react to her invitation.

"We're here to talk about Sheila Rinaldi."

A small frown appeared on the woman's expertly made-up face. "She didn't show up at work today."

Jackson and I exchanged stunned glances. It hadn't occurred to us that people here wouldn't know Sheila was dead. But of course no one would inform them, since her husband was being held in custody. Jackson rallied admirably.

"I'm afraid I have bad news. Ms. Rinaldi was found dead yesterday morning."

"What?" Genuine shock twisted Ms. Hunter's face. "Sheila? How?"

"It wasn't a natural death." A racetrack-sized understatement.

"Is Larry all right?"

I found it interesting that she would ask that, instead of, say, "Did Larry do it?"

"You know her husband?"

She gave me a baffled look, as if noticing me for the first time. "Of course. He's here all the time. They were so in love." Tears sprang into her eyes. "Poor Larry."

We gave her a moment to compose herself, and when the woman had dried her tears—without somehow smudging her makeup, I might add—Jackson asked, "Is there anything you can tell us about Sheila, her relationship with other workers, for example, that might help us in our investigations?"

"I don't know what to say. She was very well liked. Efficient in her job too. I can't understand why anyone would want to harm her."

"Has she worked here long?"

"Five years."

"Do you know if she had any serious relationships before Larry?" I asked. I wasn't ready to give up the mafia angle, but Ms. Hunter wasn't likely to reveal to us if the casino employees were crooked.

"I don't know about that. You should ask Anna Jagoda. They were very good friends. I'll show you to her."

We followed Ms. Hunter down the bare concrete corridors of the employees' quarters and one floor up to the clubhouse proper. It was a different world entirely, all chrome and glass, widescreen TVs and lounge bars, shiny at first glance, but a closer look revealed fading carpets and flaking walls. All that was forgotten, however, when you saw the view through the enormous glass wall onto the racetrack itself. You couldn't see anything else, really. There wasn't even a race on, just a couple of jockeys exercising their horses, but that was enough. I was mesmerized.

"Keep up, Tracy," Jackson said, amused, and I hurried to catch up, having paused to gawp.

Betting stalls were at the back without a view to the track, a row of booths with a heavy Plexiglas wall between the customers and the clerks. TV screens showed live broadcast from races all over the country where the season was in full swing, but not many people were here to bet on them.

Only a couple of stalls were occupied at that time of day and Ms. Hunter led us to one of them, to a young woman with thick blond hair and a pretty, round face. She frowned when she saw Ms. Hunter.

"Sheila still hasn't shown up." She had a thick accent—Slavonic, I'd say.

We left the gruesome task of relaying the bad news to Ms. Hunter—and the consequent consoling too. It took quite a while before Ms. Jagoda was calm enough to talk to us, by which time most of the employees on that floor had heard the news and gathered around us.

"If we could have a quiet place to talk?" Jackson suggested politely.

Ms. Hunter led Anna and us to a small backroom—a closet, more like. Jackson asked the young woman the usual questions, but she told us that Sheila was well liked and she had no knowledge of a previous boyfriend.

"If she had, it was before I started here two years ago."

"How about regular customers? Were there any that would have given her trouble? Blamed her for their heavy losses or some such thing?"

"No, the high rollers don't come through us." Then she frowned. "But on Thursday there was a client that upset Sheila."

"What was it about?" Jackson asked, instantly alert.

"I don't know, she wouldn't tell me. But she was pale as a sheet long afterwards."

"Do you know the customer? Would you be able to identify them for us?"

"No, I didn't see the incident. But there are cameras monitoring the customers. I'm sure you could find it there."

By the time the clubhouse security had found us the correct surveillance feed, we'd talked with the rest of the employees present and they'd all said the same: Sheila was well liked and no one would want to hurt her, least of all Larry.

"Well, somebody did hurt her, and badly," I muttered to Jackson as we followed the head of security to the surveillance room on the ground floor, where banks of monitors lined one wall showing video feeds from all over the casino.

"That's why I'm pretty sure it has to be personal and not a client here. But we'll check this out anyway."

Sheila had had a busy day on Thursday. Most of the customers spent only a moment or two at her desk: placed their bets, maybe made a smiling comment about the weather—I presumed, since there was no audio—and went on their way. It was all funny-looking, as we were viewing it on high speed.

Then a tall, elegant woman in slacks and a blouse came to her desk. It began like all previous inter-actions—money was exchanged to a ticket—but then she pointed to a photo on the side of Sheila's booth and Sheila smiled and said something. The woman then retorted with anger, making Sheila stagger as if hit.

"Can we get that in regular speed, please?" Jackson requested. When the woman's face came into clear view, he had the feed paused. "Is that who I think it is?"

My heart was beating fast. "I believe it is. Hannah Williams."

Chapter Eleven

TEN MINUTES LATER WE EXITED the racetrack with a copy of the surveillance footage, Jackson with purposeful strides, me practically skipping.

"We have to tell Trevor immediately," I said when we got in the car.

"We've been employed by Travis, so we tell him first. He can tell Trevor."

"Bit weird being placed between my brothers," I noted, digging out my phone to make the call while Jackson concentrated on driving. The call went to voicemail. "Tracy here. We've found new evidence in the Williams's case that I believe requires your immediate attention," I said to the recorder, deliberately formulating it vaguely, and hung up. "Damn. I really wanted to tell him right away."

"We don't actually have evidence that Hannah Williams killed Sheila Rinaldi."

"But we have evidence that she knew the other wife existed." We'd dropped by Sheila's booth and checked the photo, which had turned out to be of Larry Williams. "I bet Hannah noticed the photo and asked why it was there, and Sheila told her he was her husband. And then Hannah said, 'No, he's *my* husband,' or something."

"But wouldn't Sheila have confronted Larry right away? Yet there he was, going to meet her as if nothing had happened."

"Maybe she did and he managed to assuage her. I mean, he has to be good at sweet-talking women. He doesn't look like much, but he has three women at the same time."

He shrugged. "Could be. But if she was on to him it would also give him a motive. Maybe she waited till Sunday morning before she accused him, and then he killed her."

"I guess. He just doesn't look like a killer."

"Maybe his charm has got to you too," Jackson teased.

I shuddered. "What I really want to know is, why would Hannah Williams hire us if she already knew about the other woman?"

"She wanted to learn all the details."

I could see that, but there had to be more. "Or she wanted an alibi for herself. If we hadn't told her about the other woman before her death, she couldn't possibly be the murderer."

Jackson frowned. "I don't like the sound of that."

My phone rang. "What do you have for me?" Travis asked.

"We have evidence that Hannah Williams knew about Sheila Rinaldi before she hired us."

"I need to see it. Can you meet me at the 70th? I'm on my way to talk with my client."

"Absolutely. Should I tell Trevor?"

"I'll decide when I've seen the evidence." And he hung up.

"I guess we'll head to the 70th, then."

The 70th Precinct was on Lawrence Avenue, a small street in North Midwood—or South Kensington, depending on how you wanted to define the neighborhoods. It was a three-story building with an ornamental limestone façade, which made it stand out among the redbrick buildings surrounding it.

We got through security with little more than a hello, as the uniformed cop at the security desk knew Jackson—this had been his precinct—and we were shown to an interview room at the end of the first floor. Travis was already there, seated behind a small table that was bolted to the floor. He looked impatient.

"Can you get my client freed?" he asked by way of greeting. I almost nodded but Jackson shook his head.

"No, but we can make the police open another line of inquiry." He took out his phone and showed the security footage to Travis.

"This was taken Thursday afternoon. It's Hannah Williams confronting Sheila Rinaldi. Timeline indicates that Mrs. Williams hired us pretty much immediately after that."

Travis looked over the footage twice. "You're saying she would've had motive to kill Ms. Rinaldi? But how would she have found out where Ms. Rinaldi lived if you hadn't told her yet?"

Jackson and I exchanged looks. "How would she be able to hire and already pay us if she's unemployed and lives in a project?" I countered.

"Explain."

I gathered my thoughts. "I think there's more to Hannah Williams than meets the eye. She has nothing but time on her hands and a husband who isn't home all that much. I bet she's been following him around for quite some time already. She knew he spent time at the racetrack—and lied about it to us—so maybe she followed him there and learned about Sheila. Then she followed her to learn where she lived."

"Then why hire you?"

"We're the diversion."

"While you were tracking her husband, she went and killed Ms. Rinaldi?"

"Yes."

Jackson frowned. "She thought he only had one woman. She must have thought he would be with Ms. Rinaldi, so why go there at all?"

"Maybe she wanted to pin the murder on him. We'd

witness that he was there at the time of the crime. Or maybe she lied about not knowing."

"She was pretty badly shocked when she learned about the second woman."

I had to admit that. "I don't trust her, is all I'm saying."

"Okay," said Travis, "you show this to Trevor, I'll talk with my client."

"Can we listen in?" I asked hopefully.

"Absolutely not."

Travis looked so horrified I thought it best not to push. We exited the small room and went to look for my other brother.

We found him on the second floor in a fairly large room filled back to back with desks. Nothing was new or in terribly good repair, but everything was functional, and that's what mattered. Trevor's desk was at the back, by the window, next to Detective Kelley's. He was leaning back in his chair, studying something on his computer screen with a frown, but he smiled when he saw us.

"Lunch date!" He got up and gave me a hug, causing the men and women around him to leer and whistle good-naturedly. "Back off, this is my baby sister."

"And you let her hang out with that one?" one of the men smirked. "He's not even a real detective."

I felt offended for Jackson, but he just grinned. "I'm

95

twice the detective you'll ever be, Romes."

"We have something you need to see," I told Trevor and Kelley, ignoring the banter. Jackson uploaded the footage on Trevor's computer and we all gathered around to watch.

"That's Mrs. Larry Williams number one talking to Sheila Rinaldi last Thursday, in case you don't recognize her."

"You're saying they knew each other?" Kelley asked.

"They knew *of* each other, at least."

"Fuck," Trevor groaned. "Why couldn't this just have been a simple case of a bigamist killing his extra wife?"

"It may yet turn out to be that," Jackson said dryly. "But in the meantime, no harm in checking on Hannah Williams. And I'd definitely check her finances."

"What do they have to do with anything?" my brother asked.

Jackson shrugged. "I have no idea. But they don't add up."

"Maybe she gambles?" I suggested, an idea forming in my head. Maybe we needed to look at this from another angle completely.

"Gambling isn't illegal," Kelley said.

"No, but it makes sense. She's from Vegas, she has no income, yet she can afford to pay us, and it would explain why she'd be at the racetrack, since it's the closest casino in these parts. She could have been onto her husband and Sheila for months, for all we know."

"Then why would she act like she had no idea in the footage?"

"Maybe until that point she wasn't sure, or she was in denial?" If someone had told me Scott was being unfaithful, I wouldn't have believed either.

"Okay, we'll look into her finances," Detective Kelley said. Her face didn't promise I'd like the results.

Trevor ran his fingers through his hair. "Let's have lunch. I can't think on an empty stomach."

"Okay, but not at Scott's place."

We ended up at Scott's place.

After lunch—during which I managed not to see a glimpse of Scott, though the anticipation, or fear, of it almost made me lose my appetite—we went through the police reports about the crime scene, but the place had been clean. Too clean, Jackson noted.

"Maybe the murderer cleaned up afterwards?" I suggested, but Jackson looked doubtful.

"After such a violent crime of passion? I doubt they'd have been coherent enough."

"Well, someone did."

"Maybe it was Larry Williams? He comes 'home,' finds the place upturned, immediately suspects wife number one and doesn't want her to go to jail, so he cleans up."

"And forgets the blood-soaked rug?" I asked, doubtful.

"By that time the police have showed up and he goes outside to see what the action is about. Realizing Sheila's been found, he bolts."

"If he's protecting Hannah, it would explain why he hasn't talked yet." He'd been very close-lipped with Travis too, insisting that he'd been with Carol Marr the whole night. Problem was, the police couldn't find her to ask her about it.

The rest of the day we interviewed Sheila Rinaldi's neighbors, but no one had seen or heard anything. However, when shown Larry's photo, they recognized him as her husband and said that he was a very nice man. Everyone seemed to like him.

I was exhausted by the time I dragged myself home that evening. The murder investigation was emotionally more tasking than I'd expected, on top of which I'd risen extra early to run. My body had begun to ache all over during the afternoon and my walking was stiff.

I placed the takeout I'd bought on my way home on the kitchen table and slumped on the chair. Then I contemplated the paper bags for eternity, wondering if I was actually hungry enough to reach out and open them. I was saved by Jarod, who ambled out of his room and did it for me.

I blinked at him, bleary-eyed, and then straightened in shock, my exhaustion forgotten. "What happened to your face?"

Chapter Twelve

I STUDIED JAROD'S FACE IN HORROR. The right side was black and blue from his temple to his cheekbone. He frowned and winced when the gesture caused him pain.

"I didn't survive the encounter with Kathy's new boyfriend," he confessed, trying to keep his face as immobile as possible when he spoke, which made his speech sound a bit odd.

I inhaled in shock. "You went to see him? That was stupid of you. Brave, but stupid." Though I was kind of impressed that he'd done it. He wasn't exactly one to take initiative like that.

"Yeah." He looked bewildered for his feat.

I got up and took ice cubes from the freezer and put them in a plastic bag. Then I wrapped the bag in a towel and gave it to him. He pressed it against his face, wincing again. It was probably too late with the ice, but I had to do something.

"Have you shown your face to a doctor?"

"Nah. This'll be enough," he said, waving the ice pack. I wasn't convinced, but decided to let the matter be.

"What happened?"

"I spotted him in the hallway and thought to just walk past. The guy's, like, three times bigger than me, and it's all muscle. And then he kissed this girl who wasn't Kathy, and I—I don't know—got angry or something."

"Must have been a new experience for you," I said dryly. The past couple of weeks that he'd lived here, I hadn't witnessed him lose his temper once.

"Yeah. So I went up to him and said he shouldn't be kissing her, because he was with Kathy, and one thing led to another and before I knew what was going on, he shoved me."

"In the face?"

"No, I hit it against a bookcase when I fell."

I grimaced in sympathy. "So what are you gonna do now?"

"I think I have to, like, tell Kathy. Surely she'd like to know that the guy's not being faithful?"

"I don't think she'd believe you," I said, shaking my head.

"Why not?"

"She would think you're just being jealous. And then she'd get angry with you."

"Bummer."

"Yeah."

My own anger was rising, for Jarod, not for his ex-girlfriend. I wasn't usually an eye for an eye kind of girl, but Jarod was such a nice guy. No one got to punch—or shove—him without punishment.

"You'll have to make her see with her own eyes that he's fooling around behind her back." I knew from my experience that it really worked.

"How?"

"The way only you can. With technology."

He blinked his brown puppy eyes at me. "Good thing, then, that I stole his phone." He pulled the phone out of his back pocket and I started laughing.

"I had no idea you were such a criminal."

"It was an accident, really," he confessed, a bit bashful. "He dropped it when he shoved me and I sort of took it on reflex. He didn't notice it was gone, and I was off before I came to my senses. And then I didn't know how to give it back to him, so I just kept it."

"Let's see what he's up to, then."

The guy's name was Daryl Thompson, and we had access to his entire life through his phone, his messages, e-mails, calendar, and social media. Note to self: lock your phone with a password.

He had a really active social life—I'd be amazed if he found time for studying. And it turned out Kathy wasn't the only girlfriend he had. There were at least two more, and a score of others he merely flirted with. After a day spent on a case involving bigamy, I shouldn't have been surprised, but it still annoyed me.

"At least the guy's good looking," I muttered. The camera was full of pictures of him—and of his women, quite a few of them in the 'not safe for work' territory—yikes—and he posted an insane amount of his own pictures on social media too. The guy was in a serious Narcissus territory.

"Thanks," Jarod huffed, the first indication ever that looks mattered to him. He certainly didn't pay attention to his, barely combing his hair before he left the apartment.

I grinned. "It makes it easier to believe he can have this many women. Let's see, he's having a date tonight with Lisa at Tino's Lounge, wherever that is."

"But it's Monday."

"If you have three girlfriends to juggle, you have to make use of all the days of the week."

"So what do we do?"

I didn't have to think of it. "We send Kathy a message from him and invite her there too. That way she can witness it." I began typing the message right away, trying to emulate the style Daryl used. I think I nailed it pretty well.

"And then she'll be sad and I can console her?" He gave me a hopeful look.

"I wouldn't count on it."

"Bummer. Is there any, like, scenario where she'll take me back?"

I gave it a thought. "Can you stop thinking of computers more than her?"

He slumped. "I guess that's it, then."

I patted him on the shoulder. "I'm sure there's a girl out there who won't mind that you spend your days buried in computers. Now, let's get dressed and head to Tino's too, so we can witness everything."

"Won't he recognize me?"

"We'll go there well in advance and find a table where he can't see us. But if he does, you'll be there with a hot chick and he'll be envious."

"Who?"

"Me, you moron."

"Oh, right."

With that encouragement, I disappeared into my room to prepare for the night. Tino's was fancier than a pub, but not quite a club—I'd checked their webpage—so I went with my little black dress. It had been a while since I'd worn it—it was in fact a remnant of my brief stint as a cocktail waitress four years ago—and it had shrunk a bit—ahem—but I managed to pull the zipper up and even breathe afterwards. I gathered my shoulder-length hair into an artful mess, put on some makeup, and I was good to go.

Jarod had put on clean jeans and a button-up shirt and combed his hair. A great improvement, even with the bruised face.

"Don't you look nice."

He glanced at his clothes, as if seeing them for the first time. "Mom bought this shirt."

"I didn't doubt it for a minute."

Tino's was near the college by the Flatbush Avenue, but slightly too far from my place to walk, especially in the heels I'd put on—and which my stiff muscles were already making me regret—so we took my car. It was an elegant place with low lighting and small tables placed discreetly far apart, with potted palms between them to offer privacy. Shelves behind the bar were well stocked and jazz flowed quietly from the loudspeakers. A freshman on a date with the captain of the college football team would be impressed out of her panties in no time.

We ordered Shirley Temples, which appalled the bartender so badly I feared he'd refuse to serve us, and then found a nice table where we could observe unseen. We'd timed our arrival well, and our marks weren't here yet, so I amused myself by studying the people present. Even though it was Monday, there were quite a few couples there, all probably on first dates, judging by the nervous body language.

My brief stint as a cocktail waitress had been in a place similar to this, but instead of couples, singles had come there to mix, so the atmosphere had been different: loud, joyous, and at times even desperate.

Quite a few of the male customers had thought the waitresses were free game too—a state of affairs I'd expressed my opinion on by pouring a drink over one gropy idiot's head. I still thought it was unfair they'd fired me for it.

A man sitting at the back caught my attention, mostly because he was the only single person here. He was hidden in shadows and I couldn't see him clearly, studying the room like I was. He noticed me staring and I pulled back, embarrassed, but before I could turn my face he shifted so that the light fell on him and I recognized him.

Jonny Moreira.

"Shit." I got up. "I'll be right back."

Moreira got to his feet when I approached—a polite goon—and positively towered over me even though I was wearing heels. "Are you following me again?" I asked annoyed, but when he shook his head, amused, I was disappointed. It made me feel special to have him trail me.

"No, I'm on a date." I glanced at the empty chair before him and he smiled. "She's not here yet."

"With Suzy?" The first time I'd met him he'd been going out with an ex-girlfriend of Trevor's.

"She broke my heart," he said with mock sadness, and I huffed. It wasn't like I didn't believe his heart could be broken, but I had a better explanation.

"More like you dumped her when she wasn't the link to MacRath's operations you'd hoped she would be." Suzy's ex-husband was doing time for working for the previous Brooklyn drug lord.

He didn't deny it and sat down again, and I took the vacant seat. "So who's your date?" he asked, glancing at the direction of my table.

"Jarod's not my date."

"Yet you're dressed to kill," he observed with an appreciative smile that warmed my insides. It had been a long time since a man had given me that look.

"Thanks. This is a disguise. Jarod's my roommate and we're here to spy on his ex-girlfriend's new boyfriend on a date with another girl."

"Did the new boyfriend do his face?"

I frowned, still angry about it. "Yes."

"So he'll deserve whatever you have in store for him?"

"We invited the ex-girlfriend here too."

Moreira laughed aloud. "That'll end well."

"I know." I smiled back.

"Is that him?" He nodded behind me and I turned to look as our mark walked in with his date.

"Yes."

Daryl was exactly as large as Jarod had said—the photos hadn't really done him justice—making the blonde with him tiny in comparison. She was utterly besotted with him, staring at his face as if the answer to the ultimate question were written on it, and they hadn't even got their drinks yet.

I made to return to my table, but Moreira halted me by placing his hand on my arm.

"How's the case going?"

"You haven't spied on police reports today?"

"I've had a busy day."

I decided not to dwell on what that might involve. "Jackson and I are officially aiding Larry Williams's defense." His dark brows furrowed and I lifted my hands, appeasing. "It gives us access to the case we wouldn't otherwise have."

"And what have you learned?"

"Enough for the police to open another line of enquiry. What do you know about gambling?"

"Is that another mafia quip?"

"Touchy, are we? No, I simply need to know how one would hide winnings from authorities."

"Casinos are required to tell the IRS of all winnings larger than six hundred dollars."

That wasn't much. "So you'd have to win small but often to make money on the side?"

He nodded. "Is gambling a line of inquiry?"

"Could be." I tried to sound like we had a clue, but in truth we were shooting in the dark.

"Well, I've learned that Sheila hadn't had a serious

relationship in years, and the last one moved to Florida two years ago."

"Good to know."

Moreira glanced behind me and got up, so I followed suit. A tall woman in a red dress, all sleek curves like an Italian car, sashayed through the room. She had wavy chestnut hair that fell down her back, smoky eyes, red lips, and the attitude of someone who knew she was the hottest thing since fire.

"Wow," I said, unable to tear my eyes away from her—me and the rest of the room. Moreira flashed a smug smile, his attention on the woman.

"I know."

I left hastily before things got awkward—okay, before close proximity to her made me lose all self-confidence. There was no way she would've seen me as a rival.

"Anything new?" I asked Jarod when I reached our table.

"I think they're already leaving."

Chapter Thirteen

"NO, NO, NO," I muttered, but Jarod was right. Daryl and Lisa had barely touched their drinks, yet they were getting up. I hadn't anticipated the date would be so short, but with a girl that eager, who could blame him from escorting her to somewhere more private.

"It'll take at least ten minutes before Kathy gets here." We'd thought it would be plenty of time when we sent her the message. "We need to stall them."

"How?"

"I don't know." Our marks were already at the door, so I took Jarod by his hand and pulled him up to get him to move. "Let's go."

We hurried after the pair, but needn't have bothered. Daryl and Lisa had paused right outside the bar and were busy making out against the wall. The way he was grinding himself against her, I'd be amazed if they made it indoors before their clothes came off.

We looked away, embarrassed, and retreated towards my nearby car. "Maybe they'll keep at it long enough for Kathy to show up," I said hopefully, wondering all the same, if we should just get in the car and drive home. We could try this again another night. It wasn't like Darryl would be staying home at evenings.

But before I could dig out my car key, Jarod perked up. "I think she's already here."

He pointed at a woman approaching down the sidewalk from the opposite direction. She was a fairly small woman too—Daryl clearly had a type—with a severe page haircut in her black hair. She was dressed for a hot date in a barely-there skirt, low-plunging top, and heels so high she would break her ankles if she wasn't careful.

She didn't notice the kissing couple at first, they were hidden in the shadows, and when she did she didn't recognize them and merely swerved to the edge of the sidewalk to give them privacy. A moment later she was at the door to the bar.

"Halt her," I said to Jarod.

"How?"

"Just call her name." I gave him a small shove and he tumbled forward. To my amazement, he actually managed to act.

"Kathy, hey!" He walked to her and I followed, trying to look casual—or, you know, non-suspicious.

Kathy paused and frowned when she recognized Jarod. "What are you doing here, Jarod?" she asked in a fed-up voice. "I told you, we're not getting back together. I don't date losers." She shot a glance at his bruised face and sneered. My temper flared. Jarod's shoulders slumped.

"No, I..." I stepped to stand next to him. "I'm on a date," he managed to finish. I wrapped my arm around his like I owned him, but he barely noticed, too busy staring miserably at Kathy.

She gave me a slow once-over. "Isn't she a bit too ... old ... for you?"

Ouch.

"Women his age aren't intelligent enough for him," I countered, and to my pleasure she flushed.

Our exchange had finally made the kissing couple realize they weren't alone—or maybe they'd needed to breathe—and they turned to watch. Daryl straightened when he recognized Kathy and I gritted my teeth, absolutely sure that he would lead his date away from here as fast as he could while Kathy's back was turned. But I didn't count on his stupidity.

"Hey, Kathy," he called her, sounding almost delighted. And maybe he was. The more the merrier, or something.

"What?" she spat, swerving to him—and staggered backwards when she recognized him and realized the woman was with him.

"Daryl? What...? Who...?" She was utterly speechless. "Weren't we supposed to have a date?"

I almost felt sorry for her, she was so dejected.

"We were?"

"You sent me a message. Or did you send it to me by accident? Was it meant for her?" Her humiliation was fast turning to anger.

"I must have," Darryl said puzzled, not even trying to come up with an explanation for why he was here, kissing another woman no less—like that his phone was stolen, which would actually have been true, amazingly enough. Hadn't he even noticed it was gone? It was currently burning a hole into my handbag. I'd taken it with me in the off chance that we'd be able to give it back to him unnoticed.

Lisa leaned against him and gave Kathy a slow once-over. "Honey, who is she?" she demanded to know in a whiny voice I particularly disliked.

Kathy directed her ire at Lisa. "I'm his girlfriend, you bitch."

Lisa sneered. "I don't think so."

Nothing more was needed to ignite a row between the women. Words like "skank" and "whore" were used, and some others best not repeated. Daryl could only watch bewildered as the women got louder and louder in their anger.

It looked like our job here was done. I might go to hell for this, but I didn't particularly care at the moment. Kathy and Darryl had both hurt Jarod and deserved this.

I tugged Jarod's arm, claiming his attention. "Come on, let's go home."

He wasn't willing to leave yet, his puppy-eyes trained on the scene. "But what if Kathy needs me?"

"She might. But you don't need her."

Besides, it looked like Kathy was doing just fine. She was standing right in Lisa's face, spewing profanities at her a good girl shouldn't know. Lisa reacted by shoving Kathy in the chest, tearing the front of her top in the process.

That was it; the gloves came off. Kathy grabbed Lisa's hair and pulled, and Lisa did the same in return, and a moment later they were both hissing and screaming.

Rooted on the spot, I watched the women fight in fascinated horror. I couldn't believe it had escalated so far so fast. Jarod had an anxious look on his face, but Daryl was more pro-active. He tried to separate the women by grabbing them by their shoulders—and that was when Jarod found his chivalric side.

"Don't you touch her!" he shouted.

He lunged at Daryl and tried to pull him away from Kathy—an exercise in futility, if anything was. Side by side, the difference in their sizes was almost comical. Daryl barely glanced at Jarod when he shoved him away, making him fall backwards on the street.

I saw red.

"Why don't you pick a fight with someone your own

size!" I screamed so loud it made my throat hurt, and threw myself at him.

I was nowhere near his size either—or strength—and a heartbeat later I flew sideways when Daryl shook his arm. I fell on my knees on the sidewalk. My right knee hit something sharp, a piece of broken glass maybe, cutting deep, but I scrambled back to my feet, ignoring the pain. And instead of giving up, like any sensible person would, I went at him again.

He had managed to wedge himself between the screaming women, who were oblivious to the world outside their rage. Why they thought Daryl was worth fighting over I had no idea, but I saw my opportunity.

"This is for hurting Jarod," I shouted and barreled against Daryl with my best football tackle.

I've never been athletic, and I've definitely never played football. But Trevor had taught me the basics because he believed tackling was a skill I might need against attackers. This qualified as an attack, even if I was the one attacking.

The red haze of fury clouding my judgement, I failed to take into consideration that Daryl was a pro at being tackled. Plus, he was considerably heavier than me. I hit him in the lower mid-section, which should have winded him at least, but he barely staggered. I only managed to stun myself.

"What the fuck?"

He grabbed me from the front of my dress and lifted me up, up, up, until my feet came off the ground. The flimsy material of my LBD was no match for gravity pulling me back down, and I heard it beginning to tear. I'd stunned myself worse than I thought, because I wasn't scared—I was furious. Ignoring my uncomfortable position, I kicked at whatever was in my reach, but it had no effect other than hurting my cut knee.

And then I was free, gasping for breath, and Daryl was crumpled at my feet, unconscious. The women instantly forgot their row and kneeled by him, trying to revive him, and then they started to scream at my savior.

"Silence," Moreira barked, and to my amazement it worked. He turned to me. "Are you all right?"

"Yeah, a bit shaken." My dress was torn and my knee was bleeding. I checked for Jarod, who was standing a few feet away, staring at the scene in horrified awe, but unharmed.

"Your plan went down really well," Moreira drawled, shaking his head.

"In our defense, we weren't supposed to be here when the shit hit the fan." It made him laugh. "That was quite a punch," I added admiringly. Daryl was already recovering, but he seemed happy to stay where he was.

"Yes it was. And no, I won't teach it to you." I'd actually been about to ask that, so I slumped, disappointed. "Come, let's get you out of here before the cops come," he said, offering me his hand.

I could hear the sirens approaching and my gut fluttered in worry. It was really tempting to just take his hand and flee, but I shook my head.

"I'm a cop's daughter. I have to face the consequences of my actions."

He contemplated me for a heartbeat and then nodded. "I'll see you around, then." And he walked down the street, towards where his date was waiting, and they disappeared around the corner.

Chapter Fourteen

I WAS STANDING NEXT TO JAROD, well away from the women and Daryl, who was still lying down, when the cops arrived. They were seasoned pros who didn't need to shout and order us about just in case we were dangerous. But they didn't look too happy when Kathy and Lisa resumed their screaming, this time accusing me of attacking them.

Since my torn clothes and bleeding knee, and Jarod's bruised face made us look like victims, the cops didn't look convinced. One of them came over to Jarod and me and led us a few yards away from the screaming women so we could hear each other better.

"Okay, what happened?"

I tried to come up with as plausible an explanation as possible that wouldn't incriminate Jarod and me. "We came out of the bar and that guy and that blonde were kissing outside it. Then the black-haired woman arrived and started accusing him of being unfaithful and the girls got into fight. And then the guy got mixed in the fight and Jarod here thought he was going to hit the women so he went to help, but he wasn't a match to him, so I went in too. He shoved me and grabbed me. And then this guy came from nowhere and punched him and I was free."

"And where is that guy?"

"I have no idea." And that was the truth.

He turned to Jarod. "Is that what happened?"

I feared Jarod wouldn't be able to keep the truth in, but he was still a bit dazed, so he just nodded.

"They're so small and he's so big…"

The cop frowned, clearly seeing the scene through Jarod's eyes. "Are you under the influence?"

"No."

"Let's get that wound of yours patched up. Then we'll hear the others." I glanced at my knee and saw blood running towards my ankle in rivulets. It still didn't hurt, so I must be in shock, or high on adrenaline.

The cop led us to the patrol car and gave me a pad from the first aid kit to put on my knee. I was fixing it with tape when the other cop led the girls and Daryl there too.

"We'll just need your contact information," he was saying to them, clearly intending to let this go lightly. But he'd barely finished his sentence when Kathy spotted Jarod and me. With a furious screech, she lunged at us.

Five minutes later we were all under arrest.

There are few things as humiliating as being arrested—properly arrested with handcuffs and all—for brawling in public—I had to defend myself, didn't I?—but I can think of one: being arrested and then having your brother come to the rescue.

The cops turned out to be from the 70th Precinct too—a surprise, since it wasn't the closest station to our location—and when they heard my name, they immediately asked if I was related to Trevor. Since we looked too much alike to be anything but siblings, I thought it best to admit, and when they called in more patrol cars to transport us, they called Trevor too. He arrived before the additional cars did.

He did not look happy.

He ignored me and went to talk with the cops who had arrested us. They exchanged a few words I couldn't hear, shook their heads and laughed a bit. Then Trevor patted one of them on the shoulder, grinned, and came to us.

By then he wasn't smiling anymore.

He turned Jarod and me around without a word and opened our cuffs. "Let's move," he said, placing his hands between our shoulder blades and guiding us towards his car.

"But my car—"

"Move!"

We moved.

We got into his car and he pulled into traffic. The frown on his face was so deep I hesitated to talk, but I had to. "I think I need to go to the ER." The scratch on my knee must have been deeper than I thought, because blood was already soaking through the pad. He didn't say anything, but turned from the next crossing towards Brooklyn University Hospital.

"What the hell, Tracy?" he finally exclaimed. "Of all things, getting arrested?"

"It wasn't my fault," I said automatically.

"It never is."

My family said that often.

"Okay, maybe it was slightly my fault," I amended, but when he remained silent I had to confess. "Okay, it was totally my fault."

"Let's hear it, then."

I sighed, but before I could say anything, Jarod spoke from the back seat. "It was my fault."

My brother sneered. "That's very gentlemanly of you, but if you knew my sister longer, you'd know she's always to blame."

That stung.

"Yes, but Tracy wouldn't have been there if it weren't for me," Jarod tried, but I lifted my hand.

"Thanks, Jarod, but I'll have to take the blame for this." I gave Trevor the short version.

"So you set this Kathy up?" He didn't sound like he was cooling down yet.

"Pretty much, but in my defense we didn't anticipate

such a violent reaction." Then I reconsidered: "Although maybe we should have."

"Why?"

"She bashed Jarod's computers with a baseball bat when he wasn't paying enough attention to her."

My brother closed his eyes as if in pain. "Do you still have the phone?"

I dug it out from my bag and gave it to him without a word.

"And the mysterious passerby?"

"Jonny Moreira."

Trevor growled. He'd pretty much sworn to shoot Moreira on sight for abducting me. "What was he doing there?"

"He was on a date."

"Of course he was," he drawled. "Suzy?"

"They broke up. She wasn't useful anymore."

Trevor sneered in answer.

"You should've seen the woman," Jarod said, sounding awed.

Trevor gave me a questioning look, so I tried to give the best description I could. "Imagine Tessa if she were in touch with her sensual side."

"Now there's an image I need to get out of my mind." He pulled over outside the ER. "I'll fetch you a wheelchair."

"I'm fine." But by then my injured knee had stiffened

and I had great trouble getting out of the car. Trevor got me the chair and wheeled me into the ER.

The evening was young, and Monday was a quieter night anyway, so I was shown to an examination room immediately. I didn't have long to wait, but when the doctor showed up I wished it had been longer.

As if conjured by my earlier mention of her, my sister Theresa, Tessa for short, entered the room.

When your date night—or the simulacrum of one—lands you in the ER, covered in blood, it's generally nice to have family around. When the said family member is a qualified ER doctor, even better.

However, when she's closer to six-foot tall with the body of a supermodel—an actual supermodel, that's how she funded her med-school—and pixie-cut auburn hair—genuine color, unlike mine—and has a face that could launch wars, it takes stronger self-confidence than mine not to feel like a second class human next to her, even in the best of conditions.

Theresa was six years older than me and had worked at the University Hospital of Brooklyn ever since she'd qualified as a doctor. She'd had the mindset of a surgeon even when we were children, and she was now watching my injured knee the nurse had cleaned for her like a doctor and not like a sister—emotionally detached.

I gave her a helpless, imploring look. "Tell me the truth, Doctor, how bad is it? Will I live?"

She frowned. "Of course you will. You only need a few stitches. Did you hit your head?"

I wasn't entirely sure if the question was a sarcastic addition or a real one, but I shook the protrusion in question. She ignored me and took out a pen. "Follow this with your eyes." Other tests followed before she was satisfied that I didn't need to have my head CAT scanned.

With the help of the nurse, she then proceeded to stitch me up. Nothing really hurt yet, which I thought was a good thing, and I decided not to complain.

"Can you make it pretty?"

"The stitches? They don't need to be pretty. They'll come off in a week."

I sighed. "Yes, but I don't want to be scarred."

"Some scarring is inevitable," Tessa said, merciless. "But I'll do my best."

"So how's it going?"

"This is only the first one," she said, irritated.

"I mean with your life." Tessa and I only got in touch when there was news, and even then she usually told Mother, who told me.

She gave me a baffled look over her mask. "I'm not used to patients asking personal questions."

"But I'm your sister."

"Not on this table you aren't." She was quiet for a while, considering her words as she put more stitches on

123

my knee. "It's going fine. Angela's moved in with me and she's getting a divorce."

Tessa had shocked us—well, Trevor and me, since the rest of the family didn't know yet—when it turned out she was having an affair with a woman—a married woman at that. We hadn't known she was gay, let alone a femme fatale who'd break up a marriage.

"No woman is doing fine when she's going through a divorce," I told Tessa as kindly as I could. She occasionally had trouble understanding human emotions. "You have to pay extra attention to her."

"I do?"

"Yes."

"Very good. I'll do that, then."

The nurse and I exchanged amused glances behind Tessa's back, but I knew Tessa would do exactly as I said.

Trevor and Jarod were in the waiting room when the nurse wheeled me in. My brother was in a better mood, genuinely concerned for my wellbeing, when he helped me to his car. When we finally got home, after a detour by the bar so Jarod could drive my car back, I was exhausted. My knee had begun to hurt, and after I took the pills Tessa had given me, I pretty much passed out, barely making it to my bed.

I woke up when the lights came on in my bedroom.

Chapter Fifteen

JACKSON WAS STANDING IN the doorway in his jogging gear, arms crossed over his fine chest, glowering at me.

"You failed to show up on our morning run."

I was so sure I was having my recurring nightmare that I pulled the quilt over my head and went back to sleep. Or tried to. The cover was yanked off me, only to instantly return. I wasn't wearing any clothes to bed. I'd barely managed to remove the torn dress and my makeup the previous night. Putting PJs on had seemed like too much trouble.

"Sorry," Jackson said, embarrassed, staring at the ceiling.

"Nothing you haven't seen before, I hope." But I held the quilt to my throat. Then I frowned. "Are you really here or am I having a nightmare?"

"Gee, thanks. Get up. We still have time to go running before work."

"I can't. I'm wounded."

"Wounded?" he asked in disbelief.

I poked my leg out from under the quilt, showing the patched knee. "Wounded."

"What the hell happened?"

"Um, can I put some clothes on first?"

"Yes, of course. I'll go make coffee." He made a hasty retreat, clearly relieved to be elsewhere.

I got up and put on the comfiest clothes I could find; the mere thought of pulling tight jeans over the wound made my bones ache with anticipated pain. Then I limped to the kitchen, where Jackson had the coffee ready, and slumped on the chair by the table.

"How did you get in?"

Jarod couldn't have let him in. The door to his room was open and the room empty. He must have left really early, which could only mean yet another cyber emergency at work.

He looked smug. "You're not the only one who can pick locks."

"Yet you wouldn't teach me?"

"You didn't ask. So what happened?"

"I tried to be chivalrous and break up a fight."

"Right…"

"Why won't anyone believe me?" Sighing, vexed, I told him what had happened the previous night. The true story. When I finished he looked pained.

"If I'd been Trevor, I would've let them arrest you."

"Thanks."

"That was really stupid of you. You could've hurt yourself much worse."

"I almost did." I shuddered, remembering the pressure on my throat when Daryl had squeezed the front of my dress. Luckily the material was so flimsy he couldn't do much damage.

"It's good, then, that your personal goon was at hand." Oh, yeah, that had helped too. "What was he doing there?"

"He was on a date. Honestly. Nothing to do with me."

"Quite a coincidence that he'd be in the same bar," Jackson said, shooting his cop gaze at me—the one that made me want to confess to every crime I'd ever even contemplated committing.

"He was there before we came in. Only way he could've known about it was if he had this place bugged." I paused and looked around, instantly paranoid. "Do you think he does?"

"No. No one wants to spy on you."

"Hey!"

He just smiled, the cop gaze gone. "Do you want a day off?"

"Nah. But I can't go chasing after criminals until the stitches come off."

"Paperwork it is, then."

Really, not as fun as it sounds.

I was saved by a timely call from Trevor before we left

my apartment an hour later. Getting ready to work had been quite an operation and taken longer than normally. Have you ever tried to shower without getting a part of your body wet? Jackson managed to drive home, change into work clothes—and probably even go for a jog in between—and return to give me a lift to work before I was ready to go. I couldn't drive with my bum knee, and I wasn't sure I could survive the subway either.

Maybe I should've accepted Tessa's offer of crutches, but I'd thought they would be overkill. I could only hope the painkillers would start working soon and I'd be able to walk properly.

Jackson put Trevor's call on a speaker. "The coroner's report is here," Trevor said. "And you won't believe it. Turns out Sheila Rinaldi was shot."

"What?" we exclaimed pretty much simultaneously. But really: what?

"Coroner found a small caliber bullet in her brain. Her head was so badly smashed we didn't come to think of any other cause of death."

"So what now?"

"Now we have to find the weapon, won't we, one we didn't originally think to look for, so it could be anywhere by now." He didn't sound happy about it.

"Or it's in the dumpster by the house," I suggested helpfully.

"Yeah. Lucky me."

I smiled, happy—gleeful—that I wouldn't have to be the one doing the dumpster diving.

Jackson asked the one thing I didn't want to know: "So how did the head get smashed?"

"The coroner thinks she was dropped from a high place on her head post mortem."

I closed my eyes, warding off the image. "High place, like say, the third floor apartment fire escape?"

"Seems the most logical option, yes. It could even be that the murderer moved the dumpster first so they could drop the body straight into it, but then missed it and left the body where it fell."

Whoo boy. I might need to go throw up.

Jackson wasn't similarly affected. "What about the time of death?"

"It's between 6AM and 9AM, so Larry Williams isn't out clear yet."

"Have you talked to the second girlfriend? Will she vouch for him?"

"We still haven't been able to reach her. She's officially wanted for questioning."

"Do you mind if we go look around at her place?"

"Only if you can come up with a plausible reason to enter her apartment," Trevor said with a meaningful tone.

"We'll do our best."

Carol Marr lived in Williamsburg, in a three-story

building on a hole-in-the wall retail street. Everything looked fairly ramshackle and close to being demolished. The building adjacent to hers had its windows boarded over, and the empty lot next to that one indicated something had already been razed. Wire-net fencing enclosed the lot, so maybe something new would rise on it eventually.

Jackson pulled over and we spent a moment staring at the building. The windows of Carol Marr's apartment were dark and the curtains were open. They had been closed the last time I was here, on Sunday morning.

"I bet we could take a peek through the window if we could get on that fire escape," I suggested. I clearly hadn't learned my lesson.

"What do you mean we?" Jackson asked dryly. "You can't climb with that leg. But I can't get on that fire escape either. That awning over the restaurant window right underneath it blocks the access."

"So the door it is?"

"Yep."

For such a ramshackle building, the front door was surprisingly new and sturdy, as if it had been recently replaced because of a break-in—a theory that was instantly refuted by the fact that it wasn't locked. Or maybe they'd thought it was cheaper to keep it open than to replace the door after every break-in.

A small hallway opened from the door and Jackson

headed to the back of it instead of up the narrow stairs. My knee was giving me trouble, so I thought to wait for his return, but then he cursed heavily and I had to go take a look at what he'd found.

He was standing by a heavy metal door he'd opened. "Behold, the alley behind the building." It was a narrow, dark place, the buildings on three sides closing it in.

I peeked out. "But it only leads to that fenced-in lot," I remarked. "Larry wouldn't have got far if he came out here. And we'd have noticed if he'd tried to climb over the fence."

"There has to be a way out so these dumpsters can be emptied."

Jackson headed to the empty lot, disappearing around the corner to the right instead of left to the street. He was gone for quite some time, and when he returned he didn't look happy.

"You can get to the next street over from here."

"Meaning?"

"Meaning Larry Williams just lost his alibi. We can only vouch that he didn't come through the front door, but what if he went out through the back?"

He took out his phone and called Travis. "Your client's alibi just went up in smoke."

"Are you sure?" Travis didn't sound happy. "Because I'm about to go tell the police he has to be released because the time of death means he couldn't have made it to Gravesend and back to Williamsburg in time, especially with public transportation."

"There's a back door to the building. He could've had a car waiting on the next street over."

"Fuck." Travis didn't swear often, so he had to be really upset. "What about the woman he was with? Will she confirm the alibi?"

"We're on our way to interview her, but it may be she's not home. The police haven't been able to find her."

"Let me know the instant you do so I can move on with this." He hung up.

Jackson gave me a grim look. "I think we'd best find Carol Marr, then."

Chapter Sixteen

THE BUILDING HAD NO ELEVATOR, and my knee didn't thank me that I made it climb to the third floor. The way the stitches tugged with every step, I feared they would tear. At the very least, the wound probably wouldn't heal nicely and I would have a scar.

"Maybe you should've waited in the car."

"I've climbed this far. No point in turning back now."

The landing had three doors and Carol Marr's was the one at the end of the small hallway. Jackson knocked on it, loudly. We listened intently, but couldn't hear anything from the apartment. Instead, the door next to it opened and an old man in long johns and a thermal undershirt peeked out.

"What do you want?"

"We're looking for Miss Marr," Jackson said politely.

"She ain't home. She went to her mom for a week."

"Today?"

"Nah, Sunday."

That was a coincidence.

"Do you know where her mother lives?" I asked.

"Do I look like I care?"

"Then have you perhaps seen this man?" Jackson showed Larry's photo to him.

"Who wants to know?"

"I'm a private detective."

"Carol's a good girl," the old man said, looking angry. But he took the photo. "Yeah, I know him. Has been hanging around here lately. Bit of a weasel of a guy, if you ask me. Not good enough for her."

"Have you seen him here recently?"

"Was here on Saturday. And Sunday."

"Did he spend the night?"

"How should I know? I go to bed early." He pulled the door closed and locked it. A moment later the security chain was glided across too.

"That was useless," I noted.

"At least we know he actually came to her apartment on Saturday and didn't go out through the back right away."

"Now what?"

"Do you smell gas?"

I gave him a puzzled look. "No."

"Are you sure?" he asked with a meaningful look. "Do you smell gas coming from Miss Marr's apartment?"

"Ah, yes. I definitely smell gas."

"Good." He pulled on disposable gloves and opened the door with a few nifty moves of a credit card he slipped between the door and the jamb.

"That was great. Will you teach me that?" I said admiringly as I followed him in, putting on my gloves too.

"No."

"But you were upset that I didn't ask you to teach me how to pick locks."

"That wasn't the reason." But he wouldn't elaborate.

Carol Marr's apartment was just a largish room, with a kitchen and a bathroom. It wasn't in much better repair than the outside, but it was clean and nicely, if sparsely, furnished. It didn't take us long to go through it, and even a cursory study yielded interesting details.

"You'd think a woman who's left for a week would empty the perishables from the fridge," Jackson noted from the kitchen.

"You'd also think she'd take a toothbrush with her, let alone other toiletries," I countered from the bathroom.

We checked the freestanding wardrobe, and although we wouldn't know if anything was missing, there weren't any empty clothes hangers there.

"Well … fuck," Jackson said with emphasis. The next moment he was calling Trevor. "You're not gonna like this."

"I'm standing next to a pile of trash emptied from a dumpster. Anything is an improvement."

"Carol Marr's gone missing."

My brother was quiet for a heartbeat. "Missing as in left home with no intention of coming back and no forwarding address?" he asked hopefully.

"Missing as in left home without taking any personal items with her and not emptying the fridge."

"Fuck." He sighed. "Any signs of violence?"

"None."

"Okay, I'll send the crime scene investigators there. Don't go anywhere before the cops come."

We went back to the hallway to talk to the old man. He wouldn't open the door after the first knock, and when he did he kept the chain on.

"Yes?"

"You mentioned Miss Marr left for her mother's for a week. Did she tell this to you herself?"

"No, her man told me on Sunday morning."

"And what about on Saturday? Did you actually see the two of them together?" I asked.

"I don't spy on my neighbor." Jackson produced a ten dollar bill that the man quickly took. "No, he let himself in with his keys." And he threw the door closed.

Jackson and I exchanged glances. "What if Carol Marr had disappeared already on Saturday?"

Jackson looked grim. "That's excellent thinking. I just followed Larry here, I didn't actually see them together. So the question is, did he kill Carol too? He could've taken her body out through the back unseen."

"But why would he kill her? More importantly, why would he return the next day?"

"I have absolutely no idea."

"I say we go through her drawers again before the cops arrive," I suggested. "Maybe there's a clue."

"That's not exactly allowed."

"And getting into the apartment on a false pretext is?"

He grinned. "Who says it was false?" But he waved his arm towards the apartment, showing me to go in first.

We put our gloves back on and went through the drawers—the few there were. There weren't many official papers and nothing that would tell us more about her relationship with Larry.

"What kind of woman doesn't collect mementoes of her relationship?" I wondered. "A box of memories or a photo album?"

"To burn them up with the wedding photos afterwards?" Jackson quizzed, and I smiled with the fond memory. It had been a wonderful bonfire. But people didn't print out their photos anymore, so maybe Carol kept hers in her phone or computer. I glanced around, but didn't see either.

"At least we know where she works," he said a moment later, holding a pay stub. "You'll never guess."

But his excited tone suggested only one possibility. "The racetrack?"

"The racetrack. As a croupier."

"But everyone we talked with told us how happy

Larry and Sheila were together. Surely they would've noticed something."

"Maybe this was new. Maybe it was just sex."

"That would explain why there are no mementoes. But why did she have to disappear, then? Surely she was needed to testify that Larry was here the whole night."

"Maybe she wouldn't play ball."

That sounded plausible. We returned to the landing just before the cops arrived and were politely but firmly told to leave. We detoured by the dumpsters at the back, but there wasn't a body hidden there. That was a relief.

"Now what?"

"Now we return to the racetrack."

Ms. Hunter was not happy to see us back. "I thought you questioned everyone yesterday?" She was dressed in a wine-red sheath dress and looked stunning.

"This is another line of inquiry, I'm afraid. We're here to talk about Carol Marr, one of your croupiers."

She cocked a brow. "Former croupier you mean."

"Really? We weren't aware she doesn't work here anymore."

"She was fired about a week ago. Last Wednesday, if I recall. There were some discrepancies with her blackjack table. There was a client who seemed to win more often than she should have."

"And what happened to the client?"

"She was barred, of course."

Jackson nodded. "Could we get her details, please?"

"I really shouldn't reveal that information."

"If you could make an exception? This is a murder investigation, after all. I would hate to involve judges and warrants into this." Jackson said everything with a pleasant smile, but Ms. Hunter understood the threat just fine. She frowned and picked up her phone.

"I'll have to arrange clearance from the New York Gaming Commission."

While she was on the phone, I leaned into Jackson. "You just blew your chances with her."

He smiled. "I'll live."

"Really? She's almost as hot as Moreira's date."

"Was she hotter than Tessa?" He'd had a crush on my sister when they were still at school.

"Much hotter."

He grinned, but Emily Hunter finished her call just then, ending our tête-à-tête. "I have the name and address." She wrote something on a piece of paper, folded it, and handed it to Jackson. "I hope we don't have to talk about this again."

Jackson shook his head. "If matters stand the way we fear they do, the police may be here about this sooner rather than later."

We exited the office before Jackson read the paper he had been given. "Here's a surprise. Hannah Williams." My heart skipped a beat. I'd been right to suspect her.

Then he frowned. "But this is not the address we have for her."

"That's a turn of events."

"So is this." He showed me the bottom of the paper with a smug grin, where Ms. Hunter had written her name and phone number with the words 'call me' under them. "I guess you were wrong after all."

"I guess I was."

And that was a good thing, right?

We went to talk with the casino workers, who remembered Hannah Williams well. "She played a lot. Preferred Carol's table, so it wasn't a total surprise when she was fired for misconduct," the floor manager told us. "But it's difficult to believe Carol would've been involved in it voluntarily."

Maybe she was being blackmailed? When Jackson brought up Larry, no one had seen him around Carol.

"How the hell were the two of them acquainted?" I asked Jackson when we were back at the car.

"Through Hannah, maybe."

"Would you give your keys to the person who's involved you in a gambling scam?"

"Probably not. But we have no proof she was involved in it. And if she was, she definitely didn't profit from it."

That was certainly true. "We'd better find her, then."

But I had a nagging feeling we wouldn't find her alive.

Chapter Seventeen

L UNCH WAS AT SCOTT'S AGAIN, despite my protests, but Trevor had insisted. "This is close to the station. I can't be bothered to go farther than this."

"You drove all the way from Gravesend for this," I countered. "Besides, there are half a dozen eateries on this street alone you could choose from."

"Actually, I drove from home. I had to shower and change. I stank." This made me smile. "And I like the food here. Besides, it'll do you good to normalize your relationship with Scott."

That wiped the smile off my face. "I don't need to normalize anything. He cheated on me. I shouldn't have to even see him."

"Meanwhile, your hang-ups prevent you from moving on."

"I'm happy with my hang-ups, thank you very much," I growled, but I lost the argument. Thankfully, Scott wasn't behind the bar today either, so I could relax.

The four of us, Trevor, Kelley, Jackson and I, shared a booth with tall walls that offered a semblance of privacy, if not actual privacy. While we waited for our orders, we went through what we had found. Which was nothing in Trevor's and Kelley's case—except for my butterfly hairclips I'd lost in the dumpster. They were only slightly dirty, but smelled so bad even through the evidence bag that I told Trevor to throw them away. I could always go to Brownsville and buy new ones.

"There was no gun in the trash or in Sheila Rinaldi's apartment. We're waiting for a warrant to search the Williams' place," Detective Kelley told us.

"That's not the only place you need to search. The Aqueduct Racetrack had to bar Hannah Williams from gambling in their casino, and according to the New York State Gaming Commission, this is her address." Jackson handed the paper with the address—without Emily Hunter's phone number that he'd torn out, interestingly enough—to her. She read it and frowned.

"This is in Park Slope." I could understand her bafflement. I'd been amazed to find Hannah Williams allegedly lived in a very expensive neighborhood. "Is it her genuine address?"

"That's for you to find out. But if she posed as a high-roller, it could be the address is a fake."

"So what's the story about her being barred, then?" Trevor asked.

"Carol Marr, the woman Larry Williams was supposedly with on Saturday night, was a croupier at the racetrack casino. She was fired because her regular client, Hannah Williams, won more than she should have on blackjack," I explained to him.

The detectives blinked at us, not believing their ears. "So not only did Hannah Williams know Sheila Rinaldi, she knew Carol Marr as well?"

"Yes."

"And her husband was having an affair with both women?"

"Actually, I'm not sure about that," I said, having thought about it. "There was no sign of Larry Williams in Carol Marr's apartment."

"But the neighbor said he'd seen Larry around," Jackson said. "And he had a key."

"Doesn't mean they were having an affair. Perhaps he wanted to make sure she kept helping his wife to cheat at cards, or whatever. Or maybe he took the keys after disposing of her."

"Okay, back up," Kelley said. "You're saying Hannah and Larry Williams were both involved in some sort of gambling scam?"

I shrugged, because I wasn't entirely sure. "It would make more sense than if they both just happened to hang around the racetrack—he for his women, she for gambling—where she then spotted him having an affair or two, which resulted in the death of at least one of the women, maybe both."

Jackson nodded, picking up my thought experiment. "After two years in Vegas, they move here, allegedly because Larry Williams wants to be closer to his family. But could be Vegas had become too hot for them. They start their scam anew here, but things go south and people die."

"Okay," said Travis, "but why would they live in a project if they can afford a townhouse in Park Slope?"

"Well, we don't yet know it's their house, but if it is, the tenement apartment may be an attempt to fool the IRS."

"So not only a gambling scam, but a tax evasion scam too," Kelley said. "Damn. We may have to bring the Feds into this." She and Trevor didn't look happy about the prospect, but I thought it sounded cool. Maybe I could get one of those vests they wear with the FBI logo on it, or a cap...

"But let's just concentrate on solving the murder first, and possibly finding out where Carol Marr has gone to," Kelley continued. "We'll search Williams's apartment for the murder weapon and make a background check for the townhouse."

"We should try to make Larry Williams talk," Trevor added. "With the new evidence, perhaps he'd be willing to throw his wife under the bus."

"Anything for us?" Jackson asked.

"If you could contact Carol Marr's mother," Kelley

said. Technically, we worked for Travis and the Defender Service, but our goal was the same: solving the murder. "And then I think you two should set up camp outside the townhouse. If Hannah Williams shows up there, I want to know immediately."

Our food arrived. My mind occupied with the case, I didn't notice the danger that arrived with it until it was upon me—not Scott this time, the Barbie-doll he'd married. She was dressed in form-hugging green shorts, and a T-shirt with the bar's logo and a plunging neckline that revealed impressive cleavage.

I could totally have that cleavage too with a proper bra. And it would be all me. Well, except for the padding in the bra.

"Here you go. I hope you enjoy your meal," she chirped, placing our orders before us.

She didn't give me any special glances, which I took to indicate that she didn't know who I was. There wasn't a woman so self-confident she wouldn't want to measure up the ex-wife if she knew about her. I wondered why Scott hadn't told her about me. Had he even told her he'd been married before?

"Oh, we will," Trevor said with an admiring smile that was both for the woman and the food. I stared at his plate, dismayed. Even the vegetables were deep-fried.

"Meanwhile, if you ate elsewhere, you might actually avoid having triple bypass surgery before you're forty."

The woman—fine, *Nicole*—frowned, offended. "It's good, solid food."

"It's a cardiac arrest waiting to happen," I countered.

"If it's not good enough for you, perhaps you should eat elsewhere."

I smiled sweetly. "That's what I'm trying to achieve here."

She swerved around in a huff and headed to the kitchen. She wouldn't last as a waitress for long if she was this quick to take offence. All three of my companions leaned over to watch her go, eyes trained on her angrily-swinging backside.

Okay, I checked it out too, but it was really difficult not to see it.

"Really, Detective Kelley? You too?" I had to ask though.

"I appreciate a fine female form just like the next gay woman."

"I would've thought you went for a more … intellectual type."

She gave me a slow, teasing smile. "You don't know how intelligent she is."

"I have a pretty good idea." Scott had never been one for smart women, which—come to think of it—didn't really flatter me. Then again, I had been only nineteen when we met.

As if things weren't bad enough, a moment later the

man himself emerged from the kitchen and came to our table. He was wearing jeans and the bar's T-shirt, with an apron over them—and still managed to look sexy.

"I understand there's a problem with your food?"

"Why? Did the crybaby come and whine?"

"Tracy!" Trevor frowned.

"What? All I said was that the food could be healthier."

Scott sneered at me, clearly believing I was having a jealous episode. I totally wasn't. Okay, maybe a small one, but Trevor's health was important to me too.

"Other customers seem to like it just fine."

"Of course they do. Meanwhile, you could make two people out of most of them."

"That's hardly our fault," Scott huffed.

"You're not exactly helping either. But never mind, this doesn't really concern you. It's between me and my brother. Go away."

Scott clearly hadn't expected to be dismissed; his expression was so baffled. But there was only so much of his company I could stand, and I needed to eat my meal—my non-deep-fried meal, thank you very much—without throwing up.

"Are you trying to cause strife between me and Nicole?"

I rolled my eyes. "Don't flatter yourself. I only break-up one couple a week and I've already filled my quota for the week. And next week's too, most likely."

He blinked. Then he nodded at my companions, ignoring me. "Well, I hope you enjoy your lunch," he said, before returning to the kitchen.

"Happy now?" Jackson asked me.

"Ecstatic."

"So what's this about breaking-up couples?" Detective Kelley asked, and before I could prevent them, Trevor and Jackson told her the whole story of my arrest the previous night.

I did not come out great in their version.

Chapter Eighteen

AN HOUR LATER, WE HAD set up shop outside the townhouse that Hannah Williams had given as her address. It was on 6th Avenue, of all places, only three short blocks away from the agency.

"That would explain why she chose us for trailing her unfaithful husband," I noted to Jackson. "She probably sees the sign on our window when she goes to the subway."

"That still puzzles me. Why would she hire a private detective if she knew who the women were?"

We were in his car that he'd parked so we could watch both the front entrance and the entrance to the garage behind the building on the adjoining street. Not that we knew what kind of car she drove, if she even had one, but she might slip out or in on foot through there just as well.

"Maybe she genuinely didn't know about Sheila before Thursday," I mused. "She and Larry had a scheme going that involved Carol Marr. Perhaps she spent her days at the card table and Larry was a diversion, or he was there to help her count cards or whatever. And while her back was turned—figuratively or literally—he hooked up with Sheila. And then she finds out about it and hires us."

"Who killed Sheila, then?"

"My money's still on Hannah Williams. She's much larger than Sheila and could easily throw her over the fire-escape rail, whereas Larry is a short man and might've had trouble with it."

"But how would she have located Sheila without our help? Or were we simply there to provide an alibi for her husband while she killed her?"

"I don't know. If it had been me, I'd have made sure the husband took the fall for it."

"Maybe some women are more forgiving of their cheating spouses," he said with a small smile.

Fools. "Then why kill Sheila?"

"Maybe it was an accident. She went there to talk to her and the gun went off."

"At six on a Sunday morning? And why bring a gun in the first place? It's not like Sheila was a great threat."

He shrugged. "I don't know. Perhaps this has nothing to do with her husband cheating on her and everything to do with their scam."

"Carol Marr was fired and Hannah was barred. There was no scam anymore."

"Maybe it was Sheila who alerted the authorities to the scam. She notices her husband paying attention to a high-roller, gets jealous, and gets rid of her by drawing attention to Hannah."

I nodded. "And Hannah wanted revenge and killed her. And they killed Carol Marr too so she couldn't blab."

"Of all our theories, that one might actually make sense." His phone beeped and he pulled it out and checked a message from Cheryl. "She's found the owner of the townhouse."

"Who?"

"Not Hannah Williams. A holding company owns it. They've converted it to apartments and they've rented them out, but not to her."

"So it could be she doesn't even live here, that it's a bogus address?" I found that disappointing.

"Yes. But let's check the holding company first." He wrote a message to Cheryl about it. Then he Googled the names of the tenants. Two of them were a man in his late twenties and a woman in her early eighties. And the third: "Nothing. Not a trace of her online."

"That's not even possible, is it?"

"Nope. But I can't make a thorough search with the phone."

"I'll ask Jarod," I suggested. "He knows how to find the most obscure things on the web." He'd helped me before. The private security firm he worked for had a hundred-gigabyte broadband at their disposal, but better than the ultrafast connection was Jarod's ability to access accounts he shouldn't be able to.

Jackson shook his head, exasperated. "Why do I have a feeling his searches aren't exactly legal?"

"Do you need it to hold in court?"

"No." I smiled and he smiled back. "Fine. Ask him."

I took out my phone and called my housemate. He answered at once but sounded distracted. "Are you at the college?" I asked, hoping I hadn't called in the middle of a lecture. I wouldn't put it past him to answer in the classroom.

"Nah, at work. We had another emergency."

"The same cyber threat as this morning, or a different one?"

"The same. Hacktivists are blocking the website of a food production company they say uses unethical products. Makes you wonder if you're on the right side sometimes. But I'm almost done."

"Good. When you have a moment, could you check a name for me?"

"Sure."

"Alisa Strand. She should live on 6th Avenue and work for..." I checked the name from Jackson's phone. "Miller-Hollis Holdings. We found no trace of her online."

"Well, now. That should be a challenge." I could practically hear Jarod smile in anticipation.

"If nothing comes up with those parameters, check her in relation to Hannah Williams and Las Vegas."

"Okay. I'm on it." And he hung up.

"How do you want to handle this?" I asked Jackson.

"I think we should take turns watching this place. No need for both of us to be here."

"Okay." But I was kind of disappointed. I liked stakeouts with Jackson. He didn't talk much—he tended to retire to a special zone—but his company was pleasant. "As long as I can keep the car. I can't exactly traipse along the street with my knee."

"Absolutely. And you can wait here while I go check the building."

My heart skipped a beat. "But what if Hannah's there?"

"We don't know if she's Alisa Strand or connected to her. But don't worry. I'm not going into her apartment."

"Keep a line to my phone open just in case, so I can warn you if something happens."

He smiled. "Nothing will happen." But he called my phone and then put his phone in the breast pocket of his jacket.

He crossed the street to the front steps of the house we were keeping an eye on. The building was newer than the others on the long street and less pretty, with a bland brown façade and no trimmings. He took the steps to the front door, which was locked. Big surprise. Jackson didn't hesitate but pressed the buzzer of the first floor apartment, the one belonging to Alisa Strand.

"Are you insane?" I hissed into my phone, but if he heard me he didn't react.

The door didn't open, so he pressed the next buzzer. This time there was an answer. "Yes?" It sounded like an old woman.

"This is UPS. The resident in the first floor apartment isn't home and I need to leave a package. Can you open the door, please?" He sounded like a UPS guy too, carefree and a bit bored, a marked difference to his usual self-assured tone. Who knew my boss was an actor.

"Do I have to come down and sign it? Because I won't do that."

"No worries, I'll just leave the package outside their door."

"Fine." The door buzzed open.

"Thank you." But the woman had already switched off the intercom. Jackson got in.

I couldn't see him after that—and barely hear—so I concentrated on keeping an eye on the street again. No one came to the front door, but a car drove into the garage. The driver was a man though, so I didn't warn Jackson about it.

He was away for a long time for someone who wasn't checking the apartment from the inside, and I felt my stomach begin to flutter in worry. When he finally emerged it was from the garage. He got into the car and I ended the call.

"It's definitely possible to exit through the garage. But it has video surveillance, so if the police can get a warrant, we can have the security company keep an eye on it."

"Was the apartment empty?"

"I didn't go in," he said. "But I listened through the door and I didn't hear anything."

"Are you sure?" I nodded towards the front door, where a woman who looked very much like Hannah Williams was just exiting.

"Fuck."

"I guess she just didn't want to open the door."

Jackson started the engine as Mrs. Williams headed towards Flatbush Avenue on foot. "Do you think she'll take the subway there?"

"Only one way to find out."

We gave her a head start before Jackson turned the car around and followed her. She walked briskly, but a car would still overtake her pretty soon. And it seemed she would, indeed, head to the subway station, because when she reached Flatbush Avenue she turned to head to Bergen Street and the station in front of our agency.

"Get ready to get out of the car and follow her," Jackson said, and I nodded, my guts fluttering in excitement. "And don't forget to give me updates about where you're headed."

But just as Jackson slowed down and I prepared to

exit, Hannah walked past the steps leading down to the platform and entered our building instead.

"I've been here before," I said. "It ended with me being assaulted by a wanted bank robber." Not my fondest moment.

"Call Cheryl and warn her."

I was already holding my phone, so I placed the call. "A former client, potential threat, is about to enter the office. If she asks for us, tell her we'll be there any minute now. But just in case, have a pepper spray ready."

"Don't worry, I can look after myself," Cheryl said. I didn't doubt it for a second. Cheryl might be small and a decade older than Hannah Williams, but she was formidable when she got angry. But I still couldn't help worrying. If Hannah Williams was our murderer, there was no telling what she might do.

I willed Jackson to hurry.

Chapter Nineteen

JACKSON FOUND US A LUCKY free parking spot outside the 78th Precinct a street over and we were out of the car a moment later. Well, he was. My knee had stiffened while I was sitting down and I had trouble exiting.

"You go ahead. I'll catch up with you." I would've made a lousy shadow if I'd had to follow Hannah Williams.

"It may be better if we're not there at the same time. Call Trevor and give him a heads up." He broke into a run and disappeared around the corner. I limped after him, placing the call as I went.

"Not now, Tracy, we're about to enter Hannah Williams's home."

"She won't be there."

"And you know this how?"

"Because she just showed up at our office. After she came out of the building on the 6th."

"That's just great." He sounded fed-up. "What does she want?"

"I don't know. I can't walk fast enough. But maybe after you've checked the first apartment, you could get a warrant for the second."

"On what grounds?"

"How should I know? I'm not a cop."

"We can't even prove she's connected to the place, other than the info from the gaming association. The address belongs to someone else." So they'd checked it up too.

"Don't worry, we're working on it."

"Legally."

"Possibly."

He growled. "You let me know the moment you learn what she wants."

"Will do." I entered the elevator and ended the call. I was soon on the second floor. Everything seemed quiet in the hallway, but I crept—limped really silently—to the agency. The door was ajar and I peeked in—to see Cheryl shamelessly listening in on the conversation in Jackson's office through the speaker.

I tried to get in quietly, but Misty spotted me and began yapping with her usual enthusiasm, so Cheryl had to drop the intercom. It was no use pretending that I wasn't there after that.

Cheryl gave me a thorough once over, not having seen me the whole day. "What's with the sweatpants?" She was always carefully dressed and made-up, and wouldn't be caught dead in sweats.

"I have stitches in my knee," I said, sinking into the guest chair, happy to take the load off my leg. I told her the story, making her laugh so hard I feared she would smudge her makeup as tears began to fall.

The intercom beeped. "If that's Tracy there, send her in."

I went into Jackson's office, where the sight of tearful Hannah Williams met my eyes. She was slumped on the guest chair, wiping her eyes with her hand. Jackson was behind his desk, trying to keep his professional mask on, but I detected irritation around his eyes. I limped to the couch and gave him a questioning look.

Before he could say anything, Mrs. Williams gave me a horrified look. "Are you injured? It's not because of my case, is it?" Her tears began to fall again. "I knew I shouldn't have involved other people in this."

"That's okay. It was another case entirely," I said, perplexed, not understanding the waterworks at all. She had looked perfectly calm—determined even—when she headed to our office, so what had happened during the past five minutes to bring out this pitiful creature?

I dug into my messenger bag, pulled out a clean tissue, and gave it to Mrs. Williams, who started mopping her eyes with it.

"I'm sorry I'm such a mess, but I've just been told by my husband's lawyer that he won't be released yet because his alibi won't hold. I was so angry with him for having an affair, but if it had helped free him, it wouldn't have been so bad. Now I'm starting to believe that he ... that he actually did it." She looked at me with eyes so full of pain that I absolutely believed her. She was really good.

"Mrs. Williams wants to hire us again, this time to find evidence of her husband's guilt. I told her we'd do our best to get involved in the investigation." He kept his voice even, but I got the message: she didn't know that we already were.

"Of course. Is there, perhaps, anything you'd be able to tell us that would help direct our investigation?"

"Well, I found this when I went through his things this morning." She opened a large handbag she had sitting on her knee and pulled out a small black notebook. "It's my husband's."

She gave it to Jackson over the desk, who took it and gave her a reassuring smile. "I'm sure this will be really helpful."

"Will you let me know how things are progressing?" she asked, getting up.

"Absolutely." Jackson got up too and walked her out.

He'd barely closed the door after her when he rushed back into his office, grabbed his jacket from the back of his chair, and rushed out again, shouting to me as he went: "I'm going to follow her. Keep an eye on her from the window and let me know where she goes."

I limped as fast as I could to the window and attempted to see the street right below. It proved impossible, because the ledge blocked the view, so I lifted the window up and reached my upper body through the opening. Still nothing, so I climbed on the sill, knocking my injured knee as I did, making me almost curse aloud just as Hannah Williams emerged on the street. She was standing tall again, her tears wiped. She didn't look up, and didn't head back to her fancy apartment either, but briskly rounded the corner and disappeared from sight.

"I think she went down to the subway platform," I told Jackson on the phone the moment he picked up.

"Thanks. Hold the fort while I'm gone, and try to find Carol Marr's mother. And call Trevor." He hung up. A moment later I saw him round the corner too.

"That was a truly weird meeting," Cheryl said, shaking her head amazed as she came in. "And I've witnessed a lot in this office. I worked for Jackson's uncle too, you know."

I climbed back into the room, knocking my knee again. This time I did curse as a jolt of pain shot from the wound to my brain, making bright spots dance in my eyes.

"I think Hannah Williams is either a very good actor or a psychopath. Or possibly both," I said when I was able to think clearly again. I sat on Jackson's chair and called Trevor. "Have you found anything at Hannah Williams's home?"

"Nothing whatsoever. How did the meeting with her go?"

"I think she's a real psycho. She's decided to blame her husband now. And she gave us his notebook." I picked it from the table where Jackson had left it and opened it. I blinked. "This is some sort of cipher or something. The entire notebook is filled with series of numbers and letters."

"A gambling code?"

"I don't know. Could be. Would this prove he's guilty?"

"Of the gambling scam perhaps, but not the murder."

"Then why did she give it to us? Surely it would implicate her too?"

"She doesn't know that we know about her gambling," my brother reminded me. "Maybe she thinks it'll give him a plausible motive for murdering Sheila Rinaldi if we think he's gambling."

"But couldn't she just plant the weapon somewhere only he had access to, like Carol Marr's apartment, if she wanted to blame him for the murder?"

I could practically hear him shrug. "We still don't know it was her and not her husband. But you said she's a psycho. Who knows how she reasons." He sighed, sounding tired. "How's the other line of inquiry going?"

"I haven't heard from our special researcher yet."

"I'll pretend I didn't hear that."

I smiled. "Anyway, Jackson's following Hannah Williams now and she went into the subway. Could be she's headed your way."

"We'll keep an eye on her."

When the call ended, I turned to Cheryl. "I guess I'll try to locate Carol Marr's mother, then."

In the three weeks that I'd been Jackson's apprentice, I hadn't really mastered the art of a thorough computer search, but luckily Cheryl knew everything. We had Carol Marr's employee ID from her pay stub—Jackson had 'accidentally' kept it—and with that she was able to pull quite a lot of information.

Like the fact that Carol Marr's mother was dead.

"I think we can rule out that she's gone to her mother's, then," I said to Cheryl. So did this mean Larry had killed her after all? Why else would he have lied to the neighbor? "Are there any other next of kin we could contact?"

"There's a sister, but she lives in Connecticut."

"Carol might have wanted a change of scenery after losing her job."

But I wasn't holding my breath when I picked up the phone and called her sister. It took her a while to answer, and when she did I could hear children screaming in the background. Not a location I'd choose for a change of scenery. I decided to keep the call short. And the phone away from my ear. Ouch.

"No, I haven't heard from her for at least a month," the sister said after I'd introduced myself. "Why?"

"She's an eyewitness to a crime and the defense wants to interview her." I didn't want to worry her before we knew for sure something had happened to Carol Marr. "Could you ask her to contact us if you hear from her?"

"Sure." I gave her the number and hung up. I slumped in my chair. "Nothing."

"These things don't happen as fast in real life as they do on TV," Cheryl consoled me. "What you need right now is a cup of coffee and a donut to feel better. Let's go."

Chapter Twenty

COULD DO WITH FEWER DONUTS in my life, but this was a special case, so a few moments later—ok, a slow limping later—I parked myself on the small terrace outside the Doughnut Plant across the street with Misty while Cheryl went to fetch us all the gooey goodness. As I waited I leafed through Larry Williams' notebook I'd taken with me, but it made no more sense to me now than it had earlier.

"Anything interesting in there?"

I really shouldn't have been surprised to see Jonny Moreira taking a seat on the chair next to me, but I was. He leaned down to scratch Misty's head and she preened happily for him.

"She's doing well," he noted.

"You're not getting her back." He had originally adopted Misty to aid his boss's nefarious plans, but Jackson and I had rescued the dog and given her to Cheryl.

He smiled, straightening. "I'm not trying to. Why so suspicious?"

"I wonder."

"Does that have to do with the case?" He pointed at the notebook.

"Yes, but it doesn't tell us who killed your cousin. It doesn't tell us anything," I added, disgusted with the stupid book. "It's in code."

"May I see?" I handed the book over. It wasn't like he could make the case more messed up than it already was. He leafed through it like I had, frowning. "If this is about the gambling angle you mentioned, I'd say someone's been counting cards."

My brows shot up. "I thought you'd have to be one of those savant types to count cards." And Larry Williams hadn't struck me as one. Then again, he had to be some kind of smart to pull off the scam in the first place. If he was involved. This could be Hannah's notebook just as well. We only had her word it belonged to her husband.

"It's easier if you can do it in your head, especially if you're at the table playing yourself. You can't keep a book then. But if you have a partner this might work." He gave the book back. "Was that helpful?"

I frowned, my theories collapsing one after another in my head. "This case officially stopped making sense ages ago, so I have no idea."

"But a gambling scam is why Sheila was killed?"

"She might have exposed it and got killed because of it, but it's just the most plausible explanation. We still have no idea who killed her or where the weapon is."

"I thought her head was ... bashed." He looked pained, and I sympathized.

"Turned out she was shot." I decided not to mention that she'd been dropped from a high place too.

He blinked at me slowly. Then blinked again. "You're right. This is a mess of a case." He noticed Cheryl exiting the shop and got up. "So how did it go last night?"

I sighed. "We were arrested."

He grinned. "Aren't you a criminal. Bailed out?"

"Nah, my brother came to the rescue and he had Jarod and me freed."

This made him laugh aloud. "Maybe next time you'll think twice before going against a guy that big." With that, he headed down the street and soon disappeared around the corner.

"Was that the nice young man who gave me Misty?" Cheryl asked, placing her tray on the table on my other side. She'd been really taken with him when he came over to bring Misty's papers, and had remained so even though I'd told her who he was. But he was good looking and had been on his best behavior, so who was I to blame her for it. And he seemed to have a way with middle-aged women, because Cheryl wasn't the only one to call him nice.

"What did he want?"

I sighed. "I wish I knew."

We were halfway through demolishing the full tray of

donuts—Cheryl had gone nuts with the selection—green tea flavored glazing, anyone?—when Jarod called.

"I have the information you need. Can you come over?"

"I can, but I'd rather not. My knee is giving me enough trouble as is."

"I'll come to you, then. Are you at the office?" I said yes and he hung up.

We were back at the agency, feeling slightly nauseous—okay, really nauseous; I shouldn't have eaten that third donut—when Jarod showed up. His face looked worse than the previous day, and Cheryl went into instant mother-hen mode over it. But he didn't seem to be suffering, and his eyes were shining with excitement. We gathered around Cheryl's computer and he uploaded documents from an USB-stick.

"Okay, this is Miller-Hollis Holdings. It's a pretty obscure company with offshore accounts and subsidiaries that only exist on paper. But listen to this: the one thing in common with them is that Alisa Strand sits on the boards of all of them. She's the only named member, actually."

"And who is she?"

"No one. She doesn't exist except on paper."

My shoulders slumped. "Great. So how do we prove she's connected with Hannah Williams?"

"That was slightly trickier," Jarod said, looking

pleased with himself. "But I cracked it." He opened a new document. "Turns out, Miller-Hollis Holding was originally based in Las Vegas. Hannah Williams came under scrutiny of the gambling officials there, and she gave as her occupation personal assistant to Alisa Strand."

"Who doesn't, in fact, exist."

"Exactly. So I dug a little deeper and it turned out that every large transaction Alisa Strand made in Las Vegas was handled by Hannah Williams."

I nodded, impressed. "And what about the property here?"

"Miller-Hollis bought it two years ago when the company relocated here, converted the house into three apartments and rented out two of them, perfectly legitimately. And then one apartment was rented to Alisa Strand."

"Who still doesn't exist. So who lives there?"

"I don't know."

"Is Hannah Williams still listed as her assistant?"

"No."

"Shit." I drew a deep breath, trying to clear my head. "Okay, great job. I'll call my brother and have him decide what to do with this info. You did come by it legally, right?"

"I didn't have to hack into anything. But if you want info on those offshore accounts..." He looked hopeful.

I shook my head at him as I called Trevor. "What?" he practically barked. "Hannah Williams didn't show up here."

"Not yet. Jackson sent me a message and told me that she's pretty much travelling around Brooklyn. Either she knows he's following her or she has a suspicious mind. But never mind that, I have information for you." I told him what Jarod had found. "Is it enough to get a search warrant?"

"I can try, but I doubt it. But it's enough to contact Las Vegas police and ask about her."

"You do that. And let me know if Jackson shows up."

After the call ended, I was left kicking my heels. I wanted to do something, but I was out of options. When Travis called I was happy for the diversion.

"Do you have anything to get my client free?"

"No. His alibi has disappeared from the face of the Earth. And now his wife is trying to implicate him after all."

"For the murder?"

"Or the gambling scam she or both of them were running."

"But you have nothing that would implicate my client either?"

"I have his notebook that contains code for counting cards."

"If it's not about the murder I don't have to care. The

police have to charge him for the murder by the end of the day or he'll go free."

"There's the little matter of bigamy too."

"He can be bailed for that, and the gambling scam too, for that matter—if he can find the money."

"It may be there's plenty of money." I told him about the holding company.

"I could try to get the warrant for you," he instantly suggested.

"Isn't that a conflict of interest?"

"I represent Larry Williams, not his wife."

"In that case, try it. Though Trevor is trying too."

"I'll call him." And he hung up.

I glanced at my watch. "What are the chances they'll get the warrant today?"

"Well, if your brother knows a judge, it could go fast," Cheryl said, but she didn't sound confident.

I growled. "I don't like this. I need to see what's in that apartment." I had a bad feeling about the place. "Let's go take a look."

"Are you sure it's a good idea?" Cheryl asked. Her face echoed the worry I felt.

"Not even a little." But I wasn't going to let that stop me.

In the end, Cheryl, Misty, Jarod and I all got into Cheryl's car and she drove us half a street down from Hannah's apartment. The distance wasn't far, but we'd decided that even with the dog we'd look suspicious hanging out on the street—plus my knee was killing me and I didn't want to walk.

I got out of the car, my knee be damned. "If I haven't returned in fifteen minutes, call the police."

"What do you suppose will have happened?" Cheryl asked. She still didn't think this was a good idea, but she'd insisted on tagging along.

"I don't know, but the old lady upstairs sounded cranky."

"If the police come and find you've broken into the apartment, what will you tell them?"

"That I smelled gas?"

"I hope you know what you're doing."

"Me too." If the worst happened, I'd be arrested. And this time Trevor wouldn't fast-talk me out of it.

Chapter Twenty-one

I LIMPED TO THE FRONT DOOR, cursing the tall steps and the lack of railing. Weren't there regulations about proper banisters? But that didn't lessen my determination to get into Hannah Williams' apartment.

The front door was still locked, and knowing she wasn't home, I didn't try the buzzer to her apartment—though I would've been mightily surprised if someone had answered. Instead, I pressed the one for the second floor apartment and after a fairly long wait, the old lady answered.

"What?" She sounded as cranky as the first time.

Umm... "Girl Scouts. Selling cookies." Everyone loved cookies.

Except this old lady. "No peddling. I'll set the dog on you if you don't leave immediately."

Okay...

Undeterred, I pressed the top floor buzzer, and when a man's voice answered I decided to try the Girl Scout ruse again. It couldn't fail me twice in a row.

And it didn't. "Excellent. Come on in." The door was buzzed open and I got in. I looked around for something with which to prop the door open, but there was nothing, so I had to let it close again. If the police needed to get in, they could break the door.

The hallway was plain—two shades of brown and no trimmings—and small. Most of the space was taken up by the retrofitted stairs leading up, and there was no elevator. There were two doors, one at the back that I presumed led to the garage—I decided not to go and check— and one on the left right by the entrance, that belonged to Hannah—presumably. I pressed my ear against the door and listened really hard.

I couldn't hear anything. Not a great surprise.

My heart started beating faster in nervous excitement. Was I really going to break into the apartment? What if I was caught?

But even as I dithered, I studied the lock. It was more advanced than the ones I'd practiced picking with Dad. I wasn't sure I could open it. But I would try. It wasn't like I could break the door. Not without an axe, anyway.

I turned around to check the hall, just in case there was a fire axe handy, but I wasn't so lucky. Just the same. No judge would believe I'd accidentally broken the door with an axe.

Not opening the door wasn't an option, however. Answers to everything would be there, I was sure of it. Maybe even the murder weapon—unless Hannah Williams walked around with a gun in her handbag, which was perfectly possible too. It was a large bag.

And I'd have to open the door fast, or the next thing I knew Cheryl would've called the police. I reached into my messenger bag for the case of lockpicks, and was about to pull it out when I heard the heavy steps of a man running down the stairs. The top floor resident, I presumed.

I froze for a second, not knowing what to do. I didn't want to be caught there, but I didn't want to leave either. And then he was already on the last landing and I had no choice but to hide in plain sight. I stood facing the door to Hannah's apartment and knocked loudly, as if I had every right to be there.

The man reached the hall and I turned to look. A person on a legitimate errand would. He was maybe my age, handsome in a wholesome way—good hair, clean skin, and an open smile—and dressed hipster casual in slim-fit slacks and a button-up shirt with tiny checkers. The leather shoes looked handmade, and probably cost more than I made in a month. The only thing missing was a bowtie—hence it being a casual attire.

He came to an abrupt halt when he spotted me. "Did you see Girl Scouts here?" he asked, his face eager.

"I…" Oops. "Yes. They let me in on their way out." I gestured towards the door.

He frowned, miffed. "They never got to my apartment."

Note to self: next time you try to get into a building, use a better ruse.

"They were kind of fleeing. I think they said something about a mean old lady?"

To my relief, he bought it. "Figures. That old bat is the scourge of the entire street." He flashed me his open smile. "I'm Ryan, by the way. Do you live here?"

"Tracy, and no. I'm here to see ... my friend. But she isn't answering." I knocked on the door again, louder this time.

"Alisa's your friend?"

I stiffened. "You know Alisa?" Was she real after all? That would change everything.

"No, but she's my landlady, and I'd be curious to actually meet her. I've never managed to catch her home. She seems to be a busy woman."

"Ah. Well, no, my friend is her ... housekeeper." I decided it sounded more plausible than assistant.

"Hannah?"

My heart skipped a beat in excitement. Finally, the connection. I knew I'd find it here. "Yes."

"She should be in. I'm pretty sure I saw her come in earlier today." He banged on the door too and we paused to listen.

I frowned, not believing my ears. "Is it just my imagination or is someone calling out in there?" I'd distinctly heard a muffled cry. My heart stopped completely and then resumed in a dizzying pace.

"I think you're right." He banged at the door again. "Hannah? Do you need help?"

"You don't think she's fallen and can't get up or something?" I needed a plausible cause to get in, and an injured person would do.

"It's possible. Women are always hanging curtains and stuff on ladders and then falling and breaking their necks."

I decided not to point out that A) he was being sexist, and B) no one called for help with a broken neck. "We have to get in."

"We need to call the janitor and have him open the door."

"Who's that?"

"Larry? Hannah's husband?" He gave me a suspicious look, as if I should've known that.

"Ah. There may be trouble with that. He's not ... free at the moment."

The cry came again, more clearly this time. "We have to call the fire department, then. They can open the door."

"Yes. And ambulance too, just in case." I made a show of patting my pockets. "Do you have a phone? I seem to have misplaced mine."

"I left it upstairs. I'll go make the call."

"Hurry."

I waited only for him to reach the next landing before digging out my lockpicks. I chose a couple of them at random and went to open the door. The haste made my hands shake too much and I didn't have much luck with them. I drew a deep breath and forced myself to concentrate. Another set of picks wasn't any better—I'd need a third hand to make this work.

I was seriously contemplating waiting for Ryan to return—to heck with what he would think if I asked him to help picking a lock—but then I remembered the trick Jackson had done.

I took out my purse and pulled out a card—a library card, since I didn't want to damage my only credit card. I slid it into the small crack between the door and the jamb and glided it down towards the lock while turning the handle. Nothing happened. I was getting desperate, but I tried again, with greater force this time. And behold, the door opened—so unexpectedly that I almost lost my balance tumbling in.

I didn't have time to congratulate myself. I pulled myself together, and called: "Hello? Is anyone here? Do you need help?"

This time I heard it clearly. A woman's voice was coming straight ahead and to the right. The muffled quality of the cry made me think she was gagged.

That got me moving.

"Keep shouting," I said, and headed in the direction

of the voice. She shouted again and I opened a door on the right at the end of the hall, which turned out to be the bathroom.

Even though I'd expected it on some level, the sight that met my eyes robbed me of breath. I sank slowly to my knees, welcoming the pain that shot through me from the wound. At least I knew I was awake.

A woman about my age, with tangled dark hair, was sitting in the bathtub. She was stripped to her underwear, and her hands and legs were duct taped together. Her mouth was covered with tape too. Her eyes were wild and she was screaming behind the gag, though hoarsely, as if she'd been yelling for a long time already.

"Oh my God." Ryan's breathless exclaim behind me made me recover my senses.

"Don't touch anything!"

"We need to free her!"

"I'll handle it. You go outside and direct the authorities. And call the police."

He didn't look happy, but he did as I ordered. I scrambled up and to the woman and sat on the edge of the tub. "Don't worry, the police are on their way. I'll just take this tape off."

She was shaking and my hands were clammy, so it was really difficult to get my fingers around the edge of the tape. "This will hurt," I said, as if it mattered in her current situation. I yanked the tape off. She let out a cry, but more of relief than pain.

"Are you Carol Marr?"

"Y-yes," she managed to say from the clattering of her teeth.

Relief washed over me. At least she hadn't been killed. Then she looked behind me and her face distorted in terror. Her eyes rolled and she passed out, collapsing on the bottom of the tub with a thud.

I stiffened, fear turning my bones into ice. I turned carefully, not really wanting to see what was behind me to make her faint, but not knowing was infinitely worse.

Hannah Williams was standing in the doorway, pointing a gun at me.

Chapter Twenty-two

"AREN'T YOU A CLEVER LITTLE DETECTIVE," Hannah sneered. Gone was the breathy voice of a feeble, helpless female, replaced with a cold, calculating tone. Her poise was different too; she stood straight, taking advantage of her height, and stared down at me. Her weapon didn't waver.

"Yeah," I managed to say, my eyes fixed on the gun. This was the second time in my life I'd been held at gunpoint and this time I knew to be frightened.

Scratch that. I was petrified.

"How did you find here? And so fast?"

At least she hadn't noticed us tailing her. Did that mean Jackson was near? Maybe Ryan was letting him in even as we spoke. Knowing that he would be here soon calmed me and I was able to think again.

"We've been working for your husband's defense. The casino provided the address to this place."

"It's classified information," she said, appalled, as if the casino had committed a huge crime.

"This is a murder investigation. It overrides certain secrets."

"How did you get involved in it anyway?" She sounded genuinely curious. "I only hired you to trail Larry."

I could've told her she hired us for this today, but I didn't want to aggravate her. "We were involved from the start. I found Sheila's body."

She staggered, her gun briefly lowering, only to return to point at my face. "How?"

"I followed your husband from Carol Marr's place to Sheila's that morning."

"No, he came straight home. He told me so." She sounded like a little girl now whose daddy hasn't kept his promise, petulant and baffled at the same time. The mood change made her seem slightly unhinged, as if she wasn't completely in control of herself, and I really hoped she wouldn't snap before the police arrived.

Shouldn't they be here already? And where was Jackson? He was near, wasn't he?

Then her face twisted anger. "I should kill you for lying." She cocked the weapon and I realized I was screwed. My heart was beating so hard I couldn't breathe properly.

"The police are coming," I managed to say, my voice squeaking.

My words made her pull herself together. It was almost like she'd clicked a switch, so fast was the change; the cold calculation returned. "If you are referring to Ryan, he won't be alerting anyone."

I felt nauseous. "Did you kill him?" If I'd got Ryan killed I'd never forgive myself.

"No. I knocked him unconscious. I'm not a murderer."

"But you killed Sheila Rinaldi." The accusation just came out and I tensed, fearing her reaction.

"She deserved it," she said calmly.

I hadn't expected her to admit it. "Why? Because she figured out your gambling scam?"

She huffed. "That airhead couldn't figure out a one-piece puzzle. No, she had to die because she stole my husband."

"This was about him cheating on you after all?" I have to say, I was kind of disappointed for the mundane motive. But she just sneered.

"Larry couldn't not stray if I'd tied him up. He's always had women. But this time he wanted to leave with her. He wanted to leave me and marry her." The edge of madness had returned to her voice and I prayed she wouldn't succumb to it.

"Didn't he?"

It was as if I had no control over what popped out of my mouth.

"What?"

"He was married to Sheila."

She stared at me in disbelief. "But he's married to me."

"It's not exactly a legal marriage, and he'll likely do time for it, but they went through the 'I dos.'"

I really, really shouldn't have said that. Her face distorted with fury and she stepped closer to me, the gun trained right at my face. I pulled hastily back, only to lose my balance on the tub's edge and almost falling atop the still-unconscious Carol Marr. I managed to prop a hand against the wall behind me, which left me hanging in an awkward position over her.

"You lying bitch. I should kill you for that alone."

"I'm not the one who lied to you. It was Larry." My hand was so sweaty I began to slowly glide down the tiled wall, but I didn't dare push myself back up. I barely dared to breathe.

"Oh, I'll deal with him, all right. But I'll deal with you first."

Two things happened at the same time, although I only reacted to one of them. My hand finally slipped on the tile, plunging me face first into the tub, causing me to bang my head, and Hannah discharged the weapon.

The sound was deafening in the bathroom, and I kept my head down as the bullet ricocheted from the tiled walls, landing who knows where.

"Did I hit you?"

I stilled, trying not to breathe. My face was wedged between the tub wall and the captive woman's back, so I couldn't see anything, but the hairs on the back of my neck were pointing up, reacting to the imminent threat. Hannah had to be standing right by the tub.

If you've ever tried to hold your breath when you're terrified and running on adrenaline, you know it can't be done. My lungs were screaming after only a couple of seconds, demanding I start panting, instantly.

"You're breathing, aren't you?" Hannah's voice came right above me and I stifled a whimper. "Are you injured?"

She waited for a heartbeat that felt like an eternity to my lungs. Then I heard the weapon being cocked and my heart finally stopped beating altogether. I wanted to move, to surge out of the tub, to do something, but I was petrified. I could only wait for the bullet to hit and hope it wouldn't hurt.

"Hold! Drop your weapon. Raise your hands and turn around, slowly."

I'd never heard more beautiful words in my life. The cop sounded like Jackson, but even if he was a stranger, I'd love him forever for saying them.

"No."

I froze again.

"Mrs. Williams, I will shoot you if you don't put the weapon down right now." Definitely Jackson. His tone was assertive and firm. I knew he'd come for me.

"Even if you're the fastest shot in the world, I'll still manage to shoot this one first."

There was no delay this time round. The bathroom echoed with the roar of the shots, making it impossible to hear what was happening. I pressed tightly against the bottom of the tub, marveling how nothing hurt. Had to be the adrenaline.

And then it was all over. Hands were patting me, urgently, from head to toes. "Tracy, are you all right?" Jackson's voice sounded muffled, my ears still ringing from the noise.

I opened my eyes, and I swear he was the most wonderful sight I'd ever seen. He looked panicked as he studied me for injuries.

"I don't know," I managed to say. I tried to get up, but the tub and my odd position made it impossible, so he pulled me up. Then he was hugging me as tightly as he could and I tried to hug him back, only my arms had gone numb.

"Ouch."

"Are you hurt? Did she hit you?"

"No, I think…" I turned to look at Carol Marr, who was moaning as she began to regain consciousness. Blood was running from a wound in her arm—the arm that had been closest to my head.

"She missed."

"I didn't." He looked grim.

He lifted me out of the tub, as if I didn't weigh anything, just as the police swarmed into the bathroom, their weapons pointed at us. They clearly recognized Jackson, because we weren't shot.

"It's over," Jackson said. "Get the paramedics. The one in the tub needs medical attention. The one on the floor doesn't." His voice was hard. He'd shot a woman for me.

"Thank you," I managed to say as he carried me out of the bathroom and to the living room, where more police were arriving. He just squeezed my shoulder more tightly, before lowering me into a chair.

I tried to make my brain operate again, but all I managed was to stare ahead with unseeing eyes. I got an impression of a large, elegant room, but I couldn't make my mind focus on anything.

"Is the boy alright?" I remembered to ask after a while.

"The one she knocked unconscious? Yes, he'll recover."

"Good. Good." That was about the only thing I could think of to say.

"So who is she?" he asked, when the paramedics carried the captive out of the apartment a silent eternity later.

"Carol Marr." Then I sighed. "Look, I'm sorry I broke in here, but we heard her shout and had to do something."

Jackson crouched before me and looked me in the

eyes. His were serious, mine were still off focus. "I'm just glad you're okay. But the next time you pull an idiotic stunt like this, I'll shoot you myself."

I managed a smile. "Fair enough." Then my face crumpled. "Will you go to jail now?"

"We'll see."

"Do you mind if I cry?"

A horrified look flashed across his face, but then he reached out and pulled me into a hug. "Well, I already saw you naked today. This can't be worse."

With such encouragement, what could I do but cry.

Epilogue

LARRY WILLIAMS TOLD THE POLICE everything when he learned that Hannah was dead. He'd only kept quiet because he'd been afraid of her. She'd been the brains of their gambling scams. They'd been successful too, although not as successful as her legitimate—and less legitimate—operations on the stock markets with the money she'd won at tables.

"Not that I ever saw a penny of it," he told the police. He promised to co-operate with the Feds and the IRS over them.

When Vegas had grown too hot for them, they'd moved to New York and started anew. Then he'd met Sheila and decided he wanted out. When Hannah was barred from gambling in New York, she had demanded they move again, so he had told Hannah about Sheila and that's when things went wrong.

The scene on the surveillance feed we'd witnessed had been Hannah telling Sheila she couldn't have Larry. Sheila later told him about it, and he had assured her he would leave Hannah. They'd even had plans ready.

"When Hannah killed Sheila, I knew she could do anything. I went to warn Carol, but there was only a note on her table that said she'd left for her mother's. But I knew that couldn't be. That's when I went home and told Hannah that we could leave, but it was too late, the police had already found me."

And only because his wife had hired P.I.s to follow him. She had likely meant him to take the fall for the murder from the start, but we'd never know for sure now.

Jackson was questioned for the shooting, but since it was clearly in defense of me and Carol, he wasn't charged for killing Hannah. I was questioned for breaking and entering, but Ryan testified that we had heard the woman shout, so I wasn't charged with anything either.

But that happened later. First I had to go to the ER and have Tessa stitch up my knee again. That final plunge into the tub had torn the wound open. This time round she ordered me not to move, and even forced me to take crutches. I hobbled into work on them the next day.

But that first evening I just lay on the couch at home. Mom and Dad came over and brought food, which made me cry. I'd been overly emotional ever since my rescue, but I had high hopes I'd get over it soon enough.

"There, now, pumpkin," Dad consoled me. "Everything's going to be all right." With his calm presence, and with the wonderful food Mom had made, everything kind of was.

"There's no point in asking you to quit, is there?" he asked when they were leaving.

I sighed. "I know I said I'd quit the moment people started shooting at me, but now that I've faced that, I can't. It would feel like giving up."

"Good." And the way he said it felt like praise.

"Do you want to keep the car?" Mom asked. She'd been stoic about the incident, the way she'd been stoic when Trevor did his stint in Iraq.

"Actually, if you want it, you can have it back. I don't like driving in traffic, and if I have to do a stakeout I'll just borrow it."

So she took the car.

I wasn't terribly surprised when Moreira showed up at the agency the next afternoon, while Jackson was present even. Jackson didn't try to kill him, which was more surprising. He brought flowers for Cheryl and treats for Misty, but he only shook mine and Jackson's hands. I wouldn't have minded chocolate myself.

"Thank you for finding Sheila's killer," he said gruffly. "And while I would've wanted to deal with the bastard myself, I'm happy with the outcome."

Since Jackson wasn't entirely happy he'd had to take a human life, he only grunted in answer. I smiled at Moreira.

"All in a day's work. Please, convey our condolences to her family."

"I will. She'll be buried this Saturday, if you want to attend."

Travis came by too, to tie-up the case, and he had good news for me. "I've reached an agreement with your landlord. Your rent won't go up. It is a rent stabilized apartment, after all. But there was an unfortunate loophole in the original lease that allows him to raise the rent in moderation when you switch roommates." He gave me a reproachful look for not having him check the lease when I rented the place, but I'd been in a great hurry to declare my independence after my divorce. "So the next time you have a change in housemates it'll go up the entire five hundred."

"Let's hope Jarod and I won't have a falling out, then."

Jarod and I seemed to be doing all right. He was proud he'd been able to help with the case, and worried for me for how things had turned out. He and Cheryl had called the police and Jackson—and a good thing too, because he'd lost Hannah's trail coming out of the subway. He wouldn't have been there in time.

Jarod and I were happily watching TV the next evening, eating pizza he'd brought, and chatting about this and that. We didn't have that much in common, to be honest, but we liked the same nerdy TV shows, and that was plenty when it came to roommates. He wasn't a girlfriend like Jessica had been, or the girls at work, people I could gossip with, but he was pleasant company.

Our comfortable evening was interrupted by a knock on the door. I was up before I remembered I wasn't supposed to move, and limped to the door with the help of one crutch. A familiar figure stood behind it, a woman my age with blond hair in a ponytail, her slim body dressed in a T-shirt and skinny jeans.

"Jessica! What a delightful surprise. I was just thinking that my life would be perfect if I had a girlfriend to gossip with."

"Well, your wish is fulfilled." She pointed at the suitcase behind her. "Harris and I broke up. I'm moving back here." And she swept in past me.

What the hell?

Acknowledgements

I would like to thank all my readers. Without you, these books wouldn't be possible.

And to all the usual suspects, you know who you are, thank you for your support and help.

Read a sample of the next
Tracy Hayes adventure:

Tracy Hayes, P.I. to the Rescue

Chapter One

I WAS HIT BY A STORM AS I STEPPED OUT of the elevator on my way to work in the morning. And by storm I mean the psychic whose office was next door to the detective agency I worked for, and by hit I mean pulled into a hearty hug.

And I do mean hearty: over two hundred pounds of woman, most of it in her bosom right at the level of my face. She was a very tall woman. I was only five foot six.

"Good morning, Tracy," said the storm—I mean Madam Amber.

"Gah," said I, trying to breathe.

Madam Amber's real name was Rhonda Goodwin, she was at the latter end of her forties, and nearly as wide as she was tall, especially with the layers upon layers of skirts, dresses, and scarves she always piled on herself. Cornrows reached to her waist, most of it her own hair, but there were extensions in bright colors in there too, all tied into a thick bundle with a silk scarf that covered her head. In her ears she had large golden hoops.

In short, she was a remarkable sight.

She put her hands on my shoulders, making the

dozens of thin metal bracelets in her wrists chime, and pulled back to arm's length—which still left me uncomfortably close to her impressive chest. "I feel today is a good day to read your destiny," she beamed at me, all too cheerful for such an early hour.

Well, it was nine in the morning, but I'd lost the ability to function before ten ever since I quit waitressing.

I gave her a wary look. "It is?"

This wasn't the first time Madam Amber had told me it was a good day to read my destiny, but I'd managed to avoid the ordeal so far. I didn't particularly wish to know my future. I didn't want to know what good or bad awaited me. And I especially didn't want to learn that there would be neither, that my future would be infinitely dull.

I'd only recently managed to leave behind the dull, stagnant life I'd fallen into since my marriage had failed six years ago. I was no longer Tracy Hayes, college dropout, or Tracy Hayes, unemployed waitress, or Tracy Hayes, divorcee. I was Tracy Hayes, apprentice P.I. I didn't want to find out that I might become a nobody again.

Madame Amber's smile grew impossibly wider. "Absolutely. And as it so happens, I have free time."

Arm around my shoulders, she began to guide me towards her place. I looked longingly back at the agency, but the door was closed and no one saw me being abducted. I considered yelling for help, but even though Cheryl Walker, the agency secretary, was a formidable woman, she was shorter than me and would likely lose to Madam Amber.

A shiver of horror ran down my spine when I imagined the tug of war between the women, with me as the rope.

Madam Amber's small boudoir was everything I could hope for in a psychic reader's chamber. There were soft oriental carpets, large floor pillows, and colorful drapes hanging from the walls and covering the windows. The lampshades were tasseled and cast a dim, red light to the room. The scent of incense pervaded everything, making my eyes water.

In the middle of the room sat a small table covered with a silk scarf, with chairs on both sides. At the back was a low, wide coffee table surrounded by large floor pillows. On it sat a deck of Tarot cards.

"Would you like me to read your palm, or consult the cards?"

Ummm…

"Which one is more accurate?"

Madame Amber gave a hearty laugh—really, everything about her was hearty. "This isn't an exact science, Tracy. One reveals one thing, the other something else, and all of it is true."

"In that case, I choose the palm." I didn't care either

way, but I hoped the palm reading would be faster. If I had to linger in this cloud of incense long, I might develop an acute case of asthma.

"Wonderful. I'm feeling a particular affinity towards it today."

She made me sit in the chair by the tall table and took the opposite chair herself, making the poor thing creak under her weight. Then she lit a scented candle on the table, adding another fragrance to the already full bouquet. My head began to swim.

"Please give me your hand."

I wiped my suddenly damp palm on my jeans, then rested my forearm on the table and placed my hand on hers, palm up. Her hand was warm and dry, and its brown contrasted nicely against my pasty Irish skin.

"What an interesting hand you have," she said, leaning in to study it closer. I leaned in too, wondering how she could see anything in the dim light.

"I do?"

"Oh, yes. Such wonderful things I see here."

I couldn't see anything but my ordinary palm, no matter how hard I strained my eyes. "Like what?"

"This here line…" She drew a finger over my palm, tickling me a little. "Promises long life."

I straightened, delighted. "That's good to know, what with people always trying to shoot me."

Well, twice now, and it had been a month since the

previous time, but that was twice too often for someone who was only an apprentice P.I.—even if they'd missed.

Madam Amber gave me a reproachful look. "Complications like that I cannot foresee. But if you can avoid being shot, you'll live a long life."

"Damn."

"No profanities, please." She drew a finger over another line on my palm. "And there is romance."

"There is?" I didn't know how to take that. I'd put my love life infinitely on hold when I found my husband—now ex-husband—balls deep in a groupie of his band.

"Yes. Someone tall, dark, and handsome."

Figures.

"Can you be more specific? Because I have quite a few men of that description in my life already without any romance whatsoever."

The first of them was out of romance territory by virtue of being my brother, but otherwise Travis fit the tall, dark, and handsome description perfectly. At thirty-five, he was eight years older than me, a defense lawyer at the Brooklyn Defender Service and as busy as a bee who had to hold three minimum wage jobs, but it hadn't stopped him from meddling in my life. Now that I was a P.I we actually spent more time together, as the agency occasionally investigated for the Defender Service.

The second tall, dark and handsome was my boss,

Jackson Dean. He was Travis's age—and his old school friend—and he had a nice, long-limbed, wide-shouldered body, and dark brown hair currently growing out of its cut—the man had some sort of hate relationship with hairdressers. You wouldn't instantly think he was handsome—he had a curiously unmemorable face—but once you noticed its special quality, you couldn't unsee it. His strong character shone through.

But he was out of romance territory too. He was my boss, for one. For another, he saw me only as an employee—and possibly a nuisance. And I'm sure there were other reasons too, but with my brain addled with incense, those reasons escaped me.

Then there was the even more impossible candidate who liked to pop into my life regularly to mess it up: Jonny Moreira. Definitely tall, definitely dark, and pretty handsome too. But he was a henchman to a drug lord, so even if he didn't date supermodels—which he did and I wasn't—he would be out of the question. I did have a thing for bad boys, but not quite that bad. Just because he tended to be nice to me wasn't a reason to overlook his occupation.

"I'm afraid not," said Madame Amber. "Like I said, this isn't an exact science. Mere impressions."

"Well, as long as you don't see tall, blond, and promiscuous there, I'm good." That would be my scumbag of an ex, Scott Brady, who had returned to my life recently—though I did try to keep away from him.

I often failed.

Madame Amber smiled, knowing who I meant. We'd shared our stories over multiple cups of coffee whenever she popped into the agency to have a chat with Cheryl.

"I can't see the past as well as I do the future." She pointed to another line. Her eyes grew more serious and I swallowed. This was it.

"There's a crossroads coming. Pause and think carefully when you reach it, so you won't regret your decision."

I grimaced. "I'm not very good at that."

An understatement if anything was. I'd married the scumbag only after a couple of weeks of knowing him and then followed him on tour with his band—and I definitely came to regret that. But I'd also decided to become a P.I. on a whim after losing my latest waitressing job, and despite having been shot at, twice, not to mention falling into a stinky dumpster—really not a fond memory—I hadn't regretted it yet.

"It's not in your immediate future, so you have time." She curled my palm into a fist and placed her other hand over it, closing my hand into a warm cocoon. "There, that wasn't so bad, was it?"

I gave her a hesitant smile, not knowing what to say to her. "I guess not. So how much do I owe you for this?"

Madame Amber waved her hand dismissively. "What's money between friends, eh?" I shook my head, because I didn't know. She smiled. "But if you like, there is a favor you could do for me."

Read more about Tracy and Susanna's books on www.susannashore.com

Made in United States
North Haven, CT
02 April 2022

17780184R00114